WHILE
WE WERE
WAITING

ANGELINE TREVENA

Bogus Caller Press

ALSO BY ANGELINE TREVENA

Cutting the Bloodline

The Paper Duchess Series:

The Bottle Stopper

The Matching

The Visionary

The Mothers

The Memory Trader Series:

The Smudger

The Sister

The Poisonmarch Series:

After: A Post-Apocalyptic Story Collection

1

Leanne dropped the curtain back and spun round, folding her hands behind her back.

"You should stay away from the windows," Joel said, loping into the room. "It's not like there's anything to see out there anyway."

He sidled past her, and through the archway into the kitchen diner. He'd adopted a new gait in the last few months, like something from a low-budget gangster movie. He was really beginning to play the part, beginning to believe his own hype. It was worrying.

"I was just checking to see if they'd collected the rubbish yet," Leanne said. "The bins have been out for almost a month now."

"They'll get to it when they get to it," Joel replied, pulling a box of cereal from the cupboard. "They've got more important things to worry about. Like, y'know, electricity, gas, water, food." He popped a mouthful of dry cereal into his mouth. "Don't forget

1

that they keep you fed."

"It would be nice if they could do both. The street's probably crawling with rats."

"Like I said, they'll get to it when they get to it."

"Maybe you could give them a push. But then, you're nothing but a runner for them, so I guess your influence is... limited." She didn't try to hide the venom in her voice. Joel knew what she thought of him joining that gang, and she was grateful for any opportunity to reiterate that.

"You need to remember that the gang you hate so much are the only reason you have electricity, and food, and security. Remember that old couple down the road that died last winter? In a home with no heating, no electricity, no water. Starved and froze to death. Or that guy across the street who let the despair get to him and ended it all." He curled his hand around his throat and flopped out his tongue. "And then the local dogs found him. Yum, yum, yum."

"You shouldn't talk about people like that. Someone out there loved them. Have a little respect."

Joel shrugged. "No one loves them anymore."

"You don't know that."

"No one can love you when you're dead."

"That's not true."

He shrugged again. "Well, even if they do, it doesn't matter. It doesn't mean anything. Love is pointless when they're not around anymore. And everyone dies, there's no point in tip-toeing around it. One day you'll die too, and it can either be next week of starvation, or as an old lady in a puddle of your own piss. It's your choice. Either way, you're not going to care who loves you or not at that point."

Leanne glanced up at the wall above the dining table, the large photo that used to hang there had left a ghost of its shape on the wallpaper.

"Love is hope," she whispered.

"That's a pointless emotion these days too."

"You're wrong. It's the most important."

He pushed the cereal packet back into the cupboard. "Hang onto your hope then. See how far it gets you. At least I'm doing something, not just pining for people who are never coming home. So I'll continue with what I'm doing, and I'll keep the lights on, and keep the kitchen stocked."

"There are other ways to do that."

"No, there aren't, Leanne. You either trade everything you have and then starve to death, or you work for it. And the only jobs going are with The Arcane."

"But it shouldn't be like that. You shouldn't have to join some gang."

"But it is like that. Do you see the government stepping up? Where's the army? The police? They're cowering in their homes wondering how everything turned to shit, just like all of the other losers in the world. I'm making the best of this. I'm actually doing something."

Leanne dropped her voice to a whisper. "But Joel, they kill people. You know that. Innocent people. You know the things that they've done."

"They do what has to be done. And they stepped

up when everyone else was just doing jack. What are you doing other than clinging onto hope?"

"I'm going to school, which is where you should be. You were doing well in college, enjoying your course, preparing for your future."

He snorted. "There is no future anymore. All we have is this. How long would textbooks keep us warm for?"

"There will be a future. Things will get back to normal again soon."

"What's normal anymore?"

"Well, a new kind of normal then."

Joel waved his arms above his head. "What, with the 'great despair' hanging over us all like thunderclouds? No one's doing anything, because no one can see the point in doing anything. Because everything is pointless now. The gangs took advantage of that, and that's all there is now, just taking advantage of the situation. No future, no past, just what you choose to do right now."

"If I thought like that, I couldn't even bear to drag myself from my bed in the morning."

"That would be preferable to wasting your time studying for exams that don't even exist anymore. The whole world has shut down. There's no exam boards, no one to mark your papers. No one's sitting in an office right now printing out certificates. Because they know it's useless. Pointless. That none of that matters anymore."

"It matters to me."

Joel walked over and ruffled Leanne's hair. "Well,

little sister, that doesn't mean diddly-squat. If there's no one to do your exams, it doesn't matter how important it is to you. If it doesn't exist, it doesn't exist. And nothing exists anymore. Except The Arcane."

Leanne looked at her school books spread across the table. She tidied them into a pile. "You do your thing, and I'll do mine."

"That's fine with me. Keep your delusions. I'm going out to do something real. Something that actually matters."

Leanne watched him stomp off through the living room, and winced as the front door slammed shut. The silence in the house was complete, broken only by the sound of her breathing. She looked up at the vacant space on the wall again.

"I won't just forget about you," she said aloud. "I'm here, waiting for you to come home. And I'll never stop waiting."

Taking the stairs two at a time, Leanne pushed open the door to her parents' bedroom. She paused before going inside, preparing herself for the emptiness she'd find there. Gone were the days that her mum sat at her dressing table, putting on mascara, or brushing her hair. Or when her dad lounged on the bed flicking through sports channels on the TV. All that was left was an empty room and more silence.

A stack of framed photographs leant against the wardrobe doors. Leanne crouched and flicked through them. It hurt, her whole body ached with that hurt, but it hurt even more to hide them away, to pretend nothing had changed, to pretend that the bottom hadn't been ripped out of the world.

She pulled out the large photo from the dining room and held it on her knees. They'd gone to a proper photographer on her mum's insistence. Neither she nor Joel had wanted to go, complaining that they were too old for this, that it was embarrassing. At first, the photographer had struggled to capture anything but sulky faces from the two reluctant teenagers. But he'd won them over, and they'd ended the shoot in fits of giggles. This photo, their mum's favourite, was a mass of tangled arms and legs, four faces creased in laughter. It wasn't a stiff, manufactured image, a fake portrayal of the perfect family. It was messy, and crazy, and just four people relaxed around one another. It was the essence of family life. Their family.

Leanne carried the photo back downstairs and, climbing onto a chair, returned it to its spot on the wall. She nodded, satisfied. No matter what Joel said, she wanted her parents around her. Even if it was just photographs and memories.

"I won't forget about you," she said again. "And I won't give up hope that you're coming home."

2

"Good morning, Mr Hendricks," Leanne chirped over the garden fence.

"Good morning, Leanne. Please do call me Andy, though."

Leanne smiled. She wouldn't. It felt too weird to call adults by their first names.

"How are you?" she asked.

"You know, carrying on carrying on." He gave the same response every time. It probably saved him from needing to actually consider the answer. To consider the truth.

"How are you?" he asked "And your brother?"

"Doing well, thank you." 'As well as could be expected', she added silently. She didn't dare to show Mr Hendricks anything less than positivity. It often seemed like he was on the very edge, just clinging to sanity with his fingertips. Leanne didn't want to be the one to push him over into whatever lay beyond.

"Still nice and mild for September," he said.

"October," Leanne corrected him.

"Is it October already?"

"Only just. The third."

Mr Hendricks nodded. "I missed that."

Leanne shrugged. "Not by much. I only follow the date because of school."

"How's that going?"

"Good, thank you."

"Are there many kids there?"

Leanne shook her head. "Not many. But there's not many teachers either. They've mixed us together into classes, all different ages. They had no choice really. I spend a lot of my time helping the younger ones."

"That can't be helping you very much with your own learning."

She shrugged. "I don't mind. Besides, my teacher has started recording me extra video lessons to watch at home. The stuff that's too advanced for the others in the class."

"That's very generous of them."

She looked down at the lawn. "I guess he gets lonely at home. He lost his wife." She cleared her throat. "I don't mind helping the other kids, I quite enjoy it actually."

"Maybe you could train as a teacher."

"Maybe. I've not really thought about what I want to do after school. Plenty of time to decide yet, I suppose."

"Yes. How old are you now?"

"Fifteen."

He nodded slowly. "Fifteen. A proper young lady."

"I guess."

"It's a while before I have to worry about navigating the teenage years with my girls. But if they turn out anything like you, I can be very proud."

Leanne smiled, unsure of what to say next.

Mr Hendricks looked down at the floor for a moment, before raising his gaze up to the clouds. "Do you think they're together?" he asked. "Your parents, I mean. Wherever they are, do you think they're together?"

Leanne frowned. "I'd never thought about it. I just assumed that they would be."

"They disappeared separately, didn't they?"

Leanne shook her head. "I don't know. They shared a car to work, Dad always dropped Mum off on his way. I don't know exactly when they disappeared, before or after he dropped her off. I don't know if they were together." Leanne's voice grew tight in her throat.

"I worry about it. All the time. My girls and my wife went missing separately. My wife disappeared in our own kitchen. Just like that. And the girls..." He shook his head. "I worry. Hannah's only three. She needs someone to look after her. She wouldn't be able to look after herself properly." He looked down at his shaking hands.

"I think, sometimes, that maybe they're asleep

somewhere. Like they're in a coma, or in stasis, or something like that. That they're being kept safe somewhere, until they're allowed to come back."

"Allowed." Mr Hendricks drew the word out thoughtfully. "That's an interesting choice of word. Like this was purposeful. A test. Or a punishment. Do you think we're being punished?" They stood in silence for a moment. "Do you believe in God, Leanne?"

"I honestly don't know. I'd never given it much thought before..." She drifted off, leaving her sentence unfinished.

"If God did do this, to punish us, then I don't want to validate him by believing. I want to denounce him with every breath."

"Maybe it was the devil," Leanne whispered.

"Maybe it was nothing," Mr Hendricks replied. "Maybe all of this means nothing, and we're just looking for some kind of meaning in it because that's what we do. Because otherwise we'd completely lose our minds."

Leanne stared at the scuffed toes of her trainers. "I think we have to just keep hoping. And keep remembering them. If we forget them, what do we have left?"

Mr Hendricks clapped his hands together, making Leanne jump. "You're right. As long we have the memories, there's hope. We have to hold onto that."

Despite his words, Mr Hendricks' face hadn't lightened. He didn't look hopeful in the least.

3

A warm autumn sun fell across Leanne's face, and she turned towards it, closing her eyes against the glare. She breathed in the scent of the new world. She'd lived in this street since she could remember, but it smelt different these days.

There was no smell of petrol, or freshly cut grass. No barbecues, fresh paint, weedkiller. No cleaning products or burnt toast. Beyond the stench of rotting, uncollected rubbish bags, nature had reclaimed the air for itself. Leanne could smell the morning rain lifting off the trees, the wet mud at their roots, the sweet scent of the last flowers of the year. She could smell animals, the acrid stench of their territorial markings.

She'd never thought about how humans made the world smell with their domesticity and industry. And she'd never imagined that all of it could change in less than two years.

It was a short walk to the church, and Leanne could see its tower rising above the squat suburban properties before she got to the street it actually stood on.

Its clock still turned, its bells still chimed out each hour. The small garden it sat in was still trimmed and tamed, the grass clipped short, the bushes kept tidy, the fallen leaves cleared away. Someone still cared, and the sight of it flared the light of hope inside her.

She stepped into the dimness of the foyer, the front doors thrown open, welcoming her inside. All of the walls, even parts of the low ceiling, fluttered with missing posters, with desperate pleas for loved ones to return home. Most of the posters were yellowed and curled, the paper faded and brittle. The faces of the missing people had become fuzzy and indistinguishable; eyes blurring into noses into mouths. Some had been eaten by insects, only holes where there were once names and declarations of love and pain.

She unfolded a poster from the front pocket of her jumper, smoothing out the faces and names of her parents. It matched one that fluttered in front of her, pinned to the noticeboard, and curled at the corners. She pulled out the pin and let the poster drop to the floor. She held her new one in place and pushed the pin back in, running her fingers over the pixelated images of her parents.

The discarded poster had skimmed across the

stone floor and caught against the glazed doors that led into the church. Leanne bent to retrieve it, and as she straightened up, a man approached from the other side of the glass. She stepped back as he gently pushed the door open.

"So you're the one that keeps replacing that poster," he said. "I'd been wondering. No one else seems to bother anymore." He opened the door farther and stepped through into the foyer. Crossing to a wooden bench, he sat, and patted the seat beside him. Leanne remained standing.

"I just want..." she started. "If they ever come back, I want them to know we always missed them, and never forgot them."

"I'm sure they already know."

"Because," continued Leanne, "they might come here if they come back. They might come here and see it."

"Did they attend church?"

"No. But people come to churches, don't they? When things are really shit. When they don't know what else to do."

The man gestured to the posters around them. "Yes, sometimes."

"Where do you think they are? Do you think they're in heaven?"

"Honestly? I don't know. But I'm sure that, wherever they are, they miss you, and they love you very much. They'll be hoping that you have someone looking after you. Do you have someone?"

"My brother."

He tipped his head towards the church. "Would you like to come in for a bit? I could make you some toast. We could even pray, if you wanted to."

Leanne sat on the bench next to him and stared at her hands pressed between her knees. "Is God still listening to us?"

"Even harder than ever."

She looked up at him. "Are you the vicar here? You don't wear a—" She placed her hand against her throat.

He mirrored the action. "Oh, no, I'm not the vicar. I'm just trying to keep the place going, so that it's here if anyone needs it."

"Do people come?"

He nodded. "Now and again. Less so than they used to."

Leanne looked at the triangle of sunshine that the open doors had invited in. "People are giving up."

"Or maybe they're just finding other ways of coping."

"I like that thought. What happened to the vicar? Did he disappear too?"

"No. He went to be with his sister. She lost her children, and she wasn't coping very well."

"Did you lose anyone?" Leanne ventured.

The man shook his head. "I didn't have anyone to lose." He cleared his throat and stood up. "Come back any time you want. The church will always be open. I'm Neil, by the way."

Leanne smiled. "Leanne. And, I will. Thank you."

4

As Leanne approached home, she could see Mr Hendricks in his front garden. He looked up and waved to her.

She waved back. "Good morning, Mr Hendricks."

He placed his hands on his hips. "How many times do I have to tell you to call me Andy? Formalities seem a little redundant these days."

Leanne smiled in reply.

"It's nice to have some sunshine," he said, glancing at the sky. "I guess we should make the most of it before winter."

"I guess so."

"Been out with friends?"

"I haven't spoken to any of my friends for over a year. I don't know how many of them are still around."

"A lot of people left town."

"Yeah."

"Gathering together with their families. It makes sense. I've been tempted myself. I've still got the car in the garage, just sitting there." He shrugged. "It'll never start now. Still, it's tempting to just go somewhere else and start over. Somewhere without all the memories."

"But they wouldn't know where to find you."

He looked up at his house. "It's the only thing keeping me here." He turned back at her. "It must be lonely without your friends."

"I have Joel."

"But you must miss girl company. Chatting about make-up, and hair, and boys."

Leanne looked away. "We talked about more than that, Mr Hendricks. But anyway, the things that used to be important don't really seem to matter anymore."

"Do you have a boyfriend?"

Leanne kept her head turned away as she felt her face flush. "No."

"You could. You're pretty enough to have your pick."

She shrugged, keeping her eyes fixed on the ground. "I just want to get through school."

"That's very sensible. I need to look out for you now that your parents aren't here. It's not like I have anyone else to look after."

5

Joel grunted as he placed another box down in the hallway, next to the five Leanne had already watched him bring in. When he pulled the front door open and went back outside, Leanne could see more boxes stacked on the path. He brought another one in, his legs bowing under its weight.

"What's that?" she asked.

Joel looked up the stairs at her and dragged his arm across his forehead. "Just something I've been asked to store for a while. Nothing for you to concern yourself with."

"So you're storing stuff for them now?"

"I'm doing what they ask me." He stepped back outside, and lifted another case.

Leanne came farther down the stairs and leaned over the banister for a closer look. "What's in them?"

Joel placed the box down. "I dunno. I didn't ask."

He flashed her a smile.

"They're treating you like a mug. What if it's something dangerous?"

"Like what? They're not going to put us in any danger. They keep us safe. That's why I'm doing this, because they keep us safe in return."

"What if it's stolen?"

Joel sighed. "The Arcane own everything in the town. They can't steal something that's already theirs."

"Who says everything belongs to them?"

"Show me another authority around here." He shrugged. "No one's going to say anything different."

"Because they're bullied into agreeing."

"For God's sake, Leanne, it's a few bloody boxes. The only thing you have to worry about is not tripping over them for a few days. Can you manage that?"

Leanne came down the last few stairs and slipped between Joel and the boxes. She turned back towards him and dropped into a bow. "I think I can manage that," she said.

She found bread in the kitchen, and eggs, and set about making herself breakfast. In the beginning, she'd tried to make meals like her mum had, balancing protein and vegetables and carbohydrates. But as Joel had spent more and more time away, it seemed pointless cooking full meals just for herself. And as food supplies dwindled, she saw more packeted convenience food, and less fresh food, and eating became a necessity, not the social occasion it had once been. Everything tasted the same, and she only bothered eating when her stomach rumbled.

She ignored the sound of Joel bringing in the last of the boxes, and sat herself at the dining room table, scooping textbooks out of the way to make space for her breakfast. She looked up at the wall, into the faces of her parents.

"Good morning, Mum," she whispered. "Good morning, Dad. Hope you slept well."

She ate quickly to fill the empty feeling in her stomach. At least she could get rid of that. She washed up her plate and stood it in the drying rack. Wandering back into the living room, she peered into the hallway. The house was silent; Joel had gone again. All that was left was those boxes.

She shook her head and settled back at the dining room table, pulling her textbooks towards her. She hummed to herself as she read, but the silence was somehow thicker than usual. Impenetrable.

She grabbed her phone and scrolled through the video files. She didn't care which lesson she played, she just needed sound.

Her teacher's face appeared on screen, sat in front of the crammed bookcase Leanne had got used to seeing. She knew almost every book on it, the ornaments and knick-knacks. There were spaces too. Notable spaces. Leanne glanced up at the photo of her and her family. It was just too painful for some people to be faced with reminders all the time. But for Leanne, it was a comfort. If she saw their image every day, then she wouldn't forget them. Their features wouldn't fade and become indistinguishable. And if she could remember their faces, she could recall the sounds of their voices, the way they smelt after a shower, the way they walked, and how it felt to hug them.

She turned the volume up on the video and let her teacher's voice fill the room. But she could feel the silence beyond, pressing in towards her, reaching out with thick fingers and stubby thumbs. She groaned and dropped her head into her hands. She massaged her temples.

Nothing helped. The silence persisted, and the boxes sat at the centre of it.

She wandered back into the living room and looked at them. They taunted her. With their uniformity, their meekness, their infuriating reticence. They gave nothing away; each box was identical to the next, and devoid of markings, identifiers, not even a barcode adorned them. They flaunted their innocence, their mediocrity. Leanne huffed at them and returned to her books.

Looking down at her notepad, she found it covered in idle doodles. She barely even remembered doing them. Box upon box upon box.

"That's it." She stood up, her chair squealing backwards across the floor. "I live here, and I have a right to know what's in those boxes. I have a right to know it's not something that's going to kill me."

With her hands screwed into fists, she marched through the hallway and stared at the stacked cases. She picked one up. It was heavy, and the contents rattled from side to side. She put it back down. She sniffed a corner, but it didn't smell of anything. She picked at the tape that sealed the box closed, but couldn't find a loose end that she could 'accidentally' start unravelling.

She looked down at the others, looking for an opening, a hole, a tear. What she saw was a dark patch. The contents of one of the boxes was leaking into the corner. The cardboard was soggy and mushy.

"Well," she said. "I'd better make sure it's nothing that's going to stain the carpet. Or poison me. I have a right to protect my home."

She hefted a box aside, and crouched down to the leaking one. She scratched and wriggled her fingers under the tape, tearing it back. Squinting, preparing for the worst, she pulled open the flaps and peered inside.

"Bottled water," Joel said.

Leanne lost her balance and rolled back onto her bum. "I... I thought you'd gone out," she stammered.

"I went upstairs for a nap." He nodded towards the box. "Didn't trust me, huh?"

"It's not you I don't trust. Besides, it was leaking. I had to make sure it was safe."

Joel bounced down the rest of the stairs, ruffling Leanne's hair as he passed her.

6

Leanne dragged the rake back towards her, snagging the damp leaves in its tines. There weren't too many fallen leaves, summer was stubbornly holding on, refusing to relinquish the world to autumn just yet. But the small pile of yellowing foliage filled Leanne with satisfaction.

"Good afternoon." Mr Hendrick's head appeared above the fence.

"Oh, hello, Mr Hendricks."

"Raking leaves?"

"Mum's fanatical about it. She hates dead leaves on the lawn."

He nodded. He appeared almost every time Leanne was outside, and she suspected that he watched out for her. He must be so lonely in that house by himself. A house that was once filled with the sounds of his daughters. She'd babysat for them a few times, when they'd allowed themselves a rare date night, or when the excuse of having young children hadn't let them escape a social occasion.

"It'll be winter soon," Mr Hendricks mused. "Christmas."

"Goodness, I hadn't even thought about that."

Mr Hendricks nodded. "My wife would be madly buying presents by now. She was so organised, Christmas was usually sorted by mid-November. And then I'd be out a few days before the big day, panicking that I had no idea what to buy for her. I only ever had one present to buy, and I still left it until the last minute. Why is that? She always knew what to buy for me, but I was clueless. You'd think I'd have known my wife well enough to know what she'd like for Christmas."

"Not everyone's easy to buy for. Even when you do know them well. I never know what to buy for Joel. I usually just get him vouchers."

"I usually went for jewellery in the end. Or perfume. I don't even know if she liked what I got, but she always seemed genuinely delighted when she opened it." He shook his head. "I didn't even know what she liked."

They stood in silence for a moment, and Leanne scratched through her brain for something to say. Something to break the atmosphere.

"Anyway," said Mr Hendricks, saving her, "are you and Joel going to be celebrating this year?"

"I doubt it. Last Christmas was the first one on our own, and Joel didn't even stay at home with me.

He said he couldn't bear the pretence. I'd even put the tree up, but I packed it away in the evening. I didn't mind being alone that much, I've got used to that, but it felt stupid having the tree up. I guess Christmas is just another day now. Nothing special. Just like all the others."

"Maybe we should do something together. My wife would never have let it pass by without ceremony. She'd go mad if she knew I just ignored it. Even when..." he drifted off.

"Maybe," Leanne said. She made a show of surveying the garden. "Well, it looks like this job is finished." She rested the rake against the fence. "See ya, Mr Hendricks."

He nodded. "Yeah, yeah," he said, his mind seemingly elsewhere.

7

Leanne gently pushed open the door to her parents' bedroom. She didn't go in there often, and as the door slid across the thick carpet, she wished that she'd find her parents in there, as if nothing had happened. Her dad lounging on the bed watching TV, her mum brushing her hair. But it was empty. Just like it had been each time before.

Leanne crossed to the bed and sat on the corner of it. She scooted back, bringing herself right up onto the bed, and lay down. She looked up at the ceiling. The light was concealed by an uplighter shade, a deep red to match the curtains. Her dad had bought it, and her mum always moaned to her about how dark it made the bedroom. But she put up with it with a gracious smile, and it had been there for a number of years now.

Leanne rolled over and pressed her face into the

duvet. It didn't smell of them anymore, not after more than eighteen months. It smelt dusty. It smelt like abandonment, like forgetting.

She clambered off the bed and, fuelled by anger, sadness, loneliness, she stripped it of its sheets, tossing them into a pile by the door. Once the bed was down to its mattress, she snatched up the bedding, and marched downstairs with it in her arms. Unable to see the steps beneath her, she slipped down the last few. Storming through to the kitchen, she pulled the door of the washing machine open. She stuffed the sheets in, almost toppling in with them. Liquitab. Fabric conditioner. She stabbed at the buttons to select the programme, and stumbled back as the machine began to fill with water. But she wasn't finished. Not yet.

A bucket of soapy water and a sponge, back upstairs, and she set about washing every surface. The wardrobe doors, the bedroom door, the skirting boards. The window frame, the sill, her mum's dressing table. She cleaned like a mad woman, peeling off her jumper as sweat ran down her back.

She spun around, searching for something she hadn't cleaned yet. Smudges, fluff, dust, any sign that the room was unused. That it had been closed up since—

Joel was standing in the doorway. "What the hell are you doing?"

"Cleaning."

He stepped forward and took hold of her wrist. "You're interfering. Intruding. This isn't your room.

You have no right." He dragged her towards the door.

"I'm cleaning, Joel, it was disgusting in here. Mum would never—"

"Mum isn't here."

"If we'd disappeared, she'd have never let our rooms get so filthy. She'd have cleaned them, every day, so that they were ready for us when we came back."

"Mum's not here!" he screamed. "We didn't disappear, they did. They left us. Stop trying to replace her."

"I'm not doing that. I'm just making things nice for when they come back."

He slapped her then. The sting of it matched only by the shock. She stared at him, open mouthed, her hand laid against the heat of her cheek.

"They're not coming back. You need to stop pretending that they are."

"They didn't die."

"They may as well have."

"Don't say that. They're coming back."

"No, they're not. If they could come back, they would have. They'd never leave us to fend for ourselves, not unless they were dead." He swiped a tear off his cheek, but more followed it. More and more until his shoulders heaved with sobs. "I hate this world. I hate that it took my family away from me. I hate it."

"I'm your family, Joel. I'm still here. And I need you." She wrapped her arms around him as her own hot tears started to flow.

8

Leanne dumped the black plastic sack at the edge of the pavement with the others. She looked up and down the empty road. There were bin bags here and there, outside the few houses that were still occupied. Some had been torn open by foxes, or rats, or birds, or dogs, their contents strewn across the lawns.

She prodded her own bags with a toe, empty food packets rolling out of a large tear. She looked back up the street, wondering if other people had enough to eat, and how they got their food, and what they were willing to trade for it. Despite her misgivings, Joel was looking after her. She had it easy compared to a lot of people, and she had to be grateful for that. Maybe Joel was right.

She turned and walked back up the path, only then noticing Mr Hendricks crouched on his front lawn. He had a large cardboard box next to him, and he was leaning against it as if it were the only thing propping him up.

"You should bury those," he said, nodding towards her bags of rubbish. "Stop the animals getting into it."

Leanne shrugged. "They're welcome to it. It doesn't look like we'll be getting a collection any time soon."

Mr Hendricks looked back at the box next to him. "I was thinking of getting rid of some old stuff, but now I've got it outside, I don't think I want to let it go anymore." He held out a jumper. "It still smells of her." He dropped his chin to his chest and began to cry.

Leanne automatically stepped towards him, her hand outstretched, but she stopped short. She'd never seen a man cry before.

"You should keep it all," she said gently. "For when they come back."

He looked up at her, his face streaked with tears. "Do you really think they will? I mean, really?"

She thought for a moment. "Yes. Most of the time, at least. It's not always easy. They've been gone for such a long time. Sometimes it starts to feel normal, and I have to remind myself that this isn't how things are meant to be. This isn't normal."

"I want to believe they'll come back, I really, really want to believe it, but I just don't think I do anymore. I might be able to fool myself during the day, while I can keep myself busy, but at night, when it's dark, and so, so quiet, that's when I know. That's when I know that I'm completely alone."

Leanne swallowed hard. She knew that feeling. She glanced up at her house.

"Why don't you go back to work?" she suggested. "Sticking to a routine, going to school, it really helps me. Because, if I'm looking towards the future, I can see them in it. I can see them coming back. Does that make sense?"

"My work doesn't exist anymore. Our boss disappeared along with a lot of the managers, and no one saw the point anymore."

"What did you used to do?"

He snorted. "Advertising."

"Maybe you could find a new job. Do something that people need now."

He nodded. "Maybe. It's just... It takes up most of my energy just to convince my body to get out of bed every morning. I'm not sure if I have any energy left to give to anyone else. How do you do it, Leanne? How do you find any meaning and purpose in life now?"

"I guess I just want to make sure that I have some kind of future."

He dropped his head back to his chest. "I suppose that's the difference: I know that I have no future."

"You're still alive."

He made a sound that Leanne wasn't sure was a sob or a laugh. "That's only because I can't muster up enough motivation to actually kill myself."

"Please don't say that, Mr Hendricks."

"Before this, my life was filled with love. I loved my wife, and she loved me. I loved my girls, and they loved me in that all-encompassing way that only children can. Fully trusting. Without questioning it. I had hugs and kisses, I even miss the shouting and the arguments. I miss having someone in my arms, someone against my skin. God, I just miss touching someone. And I'm not even talking about sex. Just contact. Human contact." He looked down at his hands. "Now all I have is loneliness. Endless, eternal loneliness, and it hurts like hell."

He began to sob again, his body shaking with it. Leanne placed her hand on his shoulder. He turned and straightened up, pulling her into a tight embrace.

"I miss them," he muttered. "I just miss them so much."

He held her tighter, and buried his face into her hair, kissing her head over and over. Even with her head buried in his chest, she heard Joel's shouts. Mr Hendricks pushed her away, his hands rising, held up in surrender.

Leanne turned towards Joel. He was striding across the lawn waving a knife in the air.

"Filthy paedo!" he yelled.

"Joel, no," Leanne waved her hands at him, but he kept coming.

"Don't you dare touch her."

"I'm sorry, I'm sorry." Mr Hendricks backed away.

"Get inside," Leanne said to him, stepping between him and her brother. "Get inside now. Joel, stop. Put the knife down. It's not what you think."

"Paedo!" Joel screamed again.

Mr Hendricks ran up his path, and Leanne heard his front door slam shut.

She grabbed hold of Joel's arm as he reached her, spinning him towards her.

"Did he hurt you?" he demanded.

"Of course not. You're the only one that's going to hurt anyone." She gestured towards the knife. "Where did you get that?"

"The Arcane gave it to me. Protection. And it's a good job too."

"You're such a dick, Joel."

"I should kill that dirty paedo."

"He's not a paedophile. My God, Joel. He's just lonely. He misses his family. Just like everyone else."

9

Leanne stared at her textbook, but the words had become nothing more than nonsense, blending into one another, swirling around. She sighed and closed it, looking up out of the window. She could see the playground beyond; the white lines of the basketball court, bench tables, bike racks. No one used the space anymore. Play had ceased.

"Are you ok, Leanne?"

She jumped at the sound of her teacher's voice. She nodded. "Yeah, just a bit distracted today, Sir."

"That's alright. Take a break if you want to. We all need that sometimes. Especially now."

"Do you think the world will ever get back to normal?"

He glanced at the rest of the students before sitting at the desk next to her. "What do you mean by 'normal'?"

"Y'know; people getting up and going to work. Going shopping. Going out for coffee. Like it was before. Will people come back to school, sit their exams, go to university?"

"I'm not sure things will ever go back to how they were before. I guess everyone will find a new kind of 'normal'. But too much has happened to go back. Too many people have been lost, and I don't just mean those who disappeared. People have got lost in themselves. Lost from the world. The distress runs deep, and I'm not sure it will ever go away. People will have to learn to live with it. Learn to carry it. But, right now, it's just too heavy for them."

"Do you think the gangs will always be in control?"

"Power has always been the world's most valuable currency. If the gangs can hold onto it, they will. If they're challenged, they'll fight for it. I guess it'll come down to fire power in the end."

"But what about the army? Why haven't the government stormed in and taken control back?"

He tapped his fingers on the edge of the desk. "Maybe they have, somewhere. They'd probably start with the main cities. Without any media, we have no way of knowing what's happening anywhere else. There could be battles raging in London right now, and we'd never know."

"Do you think the TV will come back on? The internet? Will people start making films and music again?"

"Probably. One day. When it makes it to the top

of the list of priorities. But right now, people need other things. They need food, and electricity, and comfort. They're wondering what the point is in waking up tomorrow, not what's showing at their local cinema." He sighed deeply. "It's just gonna take time."

10

A light drizzle had begun to fall, and the leaves that had dropped to the ground coated the wet pavement like oil. As the world dampened, the colours darkened, and it seemed like autumn was finally getting its turn.

Leanne pulled her hood up over her head and pushed her hands deep into her pockets. Each new season arrived with renewed mockery, brazenly asserting the passing of yet more time without her parents having returned. She wished she could hold the clocks still, cease the spinning of the earth, still the cycle of the moon.

She turned onto her front path and looked up at the house. She stopped. No. She wasn't ready to go in and face the emptiness again. Not yet. She turned back to the street. That's all there was these days; emptiness. Everywhere was empty. Places that were once packed with people had been stilled and silenced by this. What had happened to resilience? What had happened to standing up in the face of adversity? What had happened to carrying on? Even though things were the worst they'd ever been. It would be easy to give up. So simple to crawl into bed and never get out again. To just will yourself to die and decay. The world was in desperate need of hope, but the supplies of that seemed to have dried up completely.

Counting to three, Leanne turned back to the house, set her jaw, and marched up the path.

She glanced over at Mr Hendricks' house, a splash of colour catching her eye.

Crudely scrawled across his front door in red paint was the word 'PAEDO'. Leanne stopped, her stomach suddenly cold and empty.

"Joel," she whispered. "What did you do?"

Leanne unlocked her front door, and thundered through to the kitchen, pulling the bucket out from under the sink. She shoved it under the tap and filled it with hot water. She grabbed a scrubbing brush and a random bottle of cleaner. Her mum had a different bottles for cleaning everything; windows, kitchen tiles, bathroom taps, mould, wood, carpets, but they were essentially all the same. Surely.

She turned off the tap and dragged the bucket back outside, crossing the long grass to Mr Hendricks' house.

The paint was frustratingly stubborn, scratching off under the bristles of the brush rather than relenting to the power of whatever cleaner Leanne had used. Maybe her mum had something more powerful. If only there had been a bottle for getting rid of hateful words.

She dipped the brush again and scrubbed harder, the letters finally fading under her effort.

"Leanne."

She turned and saw Mr Hendricks at the corner of the house.

"Just stop," he said.

She scrubbed at the letters again. "I'm so sorry, Mr Hendricks. Joel's an idiot. I can't believe he did this. You don't deserve it."

"Just leave it, Leanne."

"It's alright, it's starting to shift now." She dipped the brush into the water again, sloshing it back against the door.

Mr Hendricks marched over to her and snatched the brush from her hand. "I told you to sodding leave it." He raised his arm and hurled the brush into the street. He kicked the bucket, the soapy water draining into the lawn.

11

Leanne woke as the front door slammed shut. She stretched out her legs and slowly sat up, arching her back against the aches that falling asleep on the sofa had put there.

"You're still up," said Joel, leaning against the door frame. He staggered further into the room and dropped into an armchair.

"I was waiting up for you. I was worried."

Joel gave her a lazy grin. "I'm fine."

"You're drunk. And you're not even eighteen yet."

He shrugged, raising both his hands up to the top of his head.

"It's illegal," she reminded him.

"Illegal, schmallegal. What's illegal anymore?"

"Did you spray paint Mr Hendricks' house?"

He shrugged again and laughed.

"You can't go around accusing people of that, using that word. Especially now, when everyone's so broken."

"Whatever. He's always looking at you. I've seen him. It's not right. You've even told me that it makes you uncomfortable."

"He's just lonely. He deserves our sympathy, not hurtful accusations."

Joel shrugged once more.

"What if he kills himself because of it? Because of the shame? Or the memories of his girls? How would you feel then?"

Joel leaned forward, resting his elbows on his knees. "That would be his decision, and nothing to do with me. Besides, it would give me one less thing to worry about while I'm away."

"Where are you going?" The panic that rose up inside Leanne took her by surprise. She hadn't realised how much she'd come to rely on Joel, or his position with The Arcane. She hated that she could even see the benefit in it, but to discover that she needed it, that thought sickened her.

"I have to go away for a few days on a job. It'll put me in very good favour, rise me up through the ranks, and we'll both benefit from that. You'll see."

"Where are you going?"

"You know I can't tell you that."

"Is it illegal?"

He rolled his eyes. "I told you; nothing's illegal anymore."

"Well, is it dangerous? Is it likely to get you hurt?

Or killed?" She snapped her mouth shut, biting back the words 'you're all I have left'.

"We live in dangerous times."

"'We live in dangerous times'? That's all you have to offer?" Leanne found her hands locked into fists. She pushed them down between her knees. "What about me? What am I supposed to do? Just sit here by myself wondering if I might have lost the last family I have left? I'm only fifteen, you can't leave me alone."

"I'm not leaving you alone. The Arcane will look after you. They promised me. You'll be perfectly safe."

"I'd rather fend for myself, thanks."

The lights snapped out, plunging the room into darkness, and removing all of Joel bar the faint sheen of his eyes. Leanne looked away.

"Another blackout?" came Joel's voice. "Where did you put that torch?" She heard him stand up and stumble through to the kitchen, crashing against furniture as he went.

"I thought The Arcane were meant to be keeping the lights on."

"They do most of the time. You don't know how lucky we are. But sometimes, rival gangs get in and try to take over, or just sabotage stuff. It's probably just a cut wire or a pulled plug or something. No system is ever perfect."

Another crash and Joel's face illuminated in the torchlight.

"Or foolproof," Leanne muttered.

"Just go to bed, the power will be back on by the morning."

12

"Told you the power would be back by morning," Joel said. He was slumped in the armchair, still wearing what he'd come home in the night before.

Leanne dropped her bag off her shoulder. "Did you sleep there all night?"

"Where are you going?"

"School."

"I'm getting picked up in an hour or so. Can't you wait? It's not like they care if you show up or not. It's all just make believe now anyway. Keep the kids off the streets."

"I care if I show up or not."

"Can't you wait for a bit?"

"What's wrong? Want me to wave you off? Looking for a teary farewell? Need a hug goodbye?"

Joel rubbed at his eyes. "Don't be stupid. I just thought you'd like to see me off." He pushed himself carefully to his feet, wincing as he became upright. "But, whatever. Go to school instead. Waste your life on meaningless stuff that isn't going to help you one bit."

Leanne gave him a sarcastic smile. "I will then, thanks. Enjoy your work trip. Are they paying for business class?"

"Is that what they teach you in school, is it? Clever comebacks?"

"No. Having a dick for a brother taught me that." She picked up her bag and left.

Leanne stood in the playground staring at the school. The line of empty windows stared back, reminding her of all the children that weren't here. She looked at the empty benches, the single bicycle in the rack, the toppled basketball hoop that no one had bothered to upright. The bins had been emptied and never refilled. Who was there to fill them? The corridors were empty. The world was empty.

She couldn't convince her feet to move anymore. They'd given up. They didn't see the point. And that feeling of futility was quickly travelling up her legs to infect the rest of her.

She hitched her bag further onto her shoulder and turned around, heading back towards home. But she couldn't go there, not before Joel had gone. She couldn't admit defeat, stand on the doorstep, waving him off just like he'd asked her to. She couldn't let him think that she was happy about it, that what he was doing was ok. That he was right.

She wandered aimlessly, and her feet carried her to her best friend's house. She hadn't anticipated it, and hadn't been prepared for it. She didn't fight the tears, she just let them run down her cheeks unhindered. She owed her friend that, at least.

Sophie had been the first person that she'd actually known that had disappeared. She'd even been with her when it happened. They were on their way to the library, and Sophie saw a boy she liked up ahead. He was in the year above, and she had, so far, been too shy to speak even a word to him. She ducked around the corner of the maths block, a handful of Leanne's jumper in her fist as she dragged her backwards. By the time Leanne righted herself, Sophie's grip on her had gone, as had the rest of her. She'd asked herself so many times why she hadn't moved faster, or grabbed hold of Sophie by the hand. Perhaps things would have been different.

Not much was known about the disappearances then. There'd been enough of them that the conspiracy theorists had started vlogging like crazy, but not enough that it seemed like the end of the world. Leanne had been confused rather than scared, running through all the more plausible explanations. It wasn't until two classes later, when Sophie still failed to reappear, that she had raised her hand and asked if she could speak to the headteacher.

Even then it hadn't seemed real. Lessons were suspended, and the school was searched before Sophie officially joined the list of the hundreds of other people that had disappeared without trace.

After that, the list became thousands, and then millions.

But that one disappearance was the turning point for Leanne, changing everything from an exciting curiosity to a terrifying reality. Four months later, she'd lose both her parents to it.

She looked up at Sophie's house. It was empty now. Her parents had left town just a few weeks afterwards. Leanne could still see the look on their faces as they trailed into the headteacher's office, glancing at Leanne sat outside with a look that said 'why wasn't it you instead?' She'd imagined that scenario a million times since, trying to picture the same look on her parents' faces.

She pulled her phone from her pocket. She carried it out of habit, still charging it up every night, but it rarely had any signal anymore. The odd times that it did pick up a mobile network, it still refused to connect to anything. It was little more than a relic. But there were photos on there. Hundreds of photos. Photos of back when things were normal and no one could have even imagined what was about to happen.

She remembered what her teacher had said about people needing to find a new kind of normal. Right now, she couldn't imagine what that might look like.

She pushed her phone back into her pocket, and turned back down the road. She promised herself that she wouldn't come here again. There was nothing here for her. It was an empty house. Nothing more. Of course, that's all that awaited her at home, too. She wiped her cheeks and swallowed back another ball of tears that threatened to overspill.

She wandered home slowly, taking lengthy detours around any of the places that held too many memories; corner shops, parks, bus stops. Places they had sat and shared secrets and packets of sweets. That part of her life was gone now, and there was no point in dwelling. She needed to find her new kind of normal and focus on that.

Joel had already left when she got back home, and she sighed with relief, pushing the feeling of regret deep down into her stomach. She didn't need any more of that.

She wandered through to the dining room and emptied the textbooks from her bag, slamming the heavy volumes down on top of one another, delighting in filling the house with sound, even if just for a moment. She looked up at the family photo above her.

"Might as well get some use out of the day," she said. "No point in wasting it." As an afterthought, she added "If you guys are in heaven, watch over Joel. I mean, I know you would anyway, but don't worry about me for a bit, I'll be fine. Just concentrate on him. Send him an angel, or something. If you're allowed to do stuff like that." She laughed, and it came out sounding awkward and unnatural. It seemed somehow appropriate.

She sat down and pulled one of her textbooks towards her, flipping it open. She'd bury herself in schoolwork until Joel was back. The text went in and out of focus, and she screwed her eyes shut. It didn't do any good. There was no focus to be had, her head was full of anything but school.

Admitting defeat, Leanne pushed back her chair and peered out of the kitchen window. The leaves were beginning to gather across the lawn again, clustering together in damp parcels.

She jumped as someone hammered on the front door. After a moment, the barrage of pounding came again. She froze, her hands gripping the edge of the worktop.

The letterbox squeaked open, and it took her a moment to remember the once-familiar sound. They hadn't received post in more than a year.

"Leanne?" came a voice.

She crept through to the living room, stopping short of stepping into the hall.

"Leanne? Are you in there?"

"Who is it?" she replied, with all the authority she could muster. It wasn't much.

"I've been told to look after you while Joel's away."

"I don't need anyone looking after me."

"Well, whatever then. I've got a delivery for you, so I'll just leave it out here."

The letterbox clattered shut. Through the net curtains, Leanne watched the figure walk down the path and away. She counted slowly to ten. Then she counted onwards to twenty. Then she took a deep breath and crept towards the front door. She listened. When she was satisfied it wasn't a trap, that no one was lying in wait for her, she eased the door quietly opened. She reached out and grabbed the bag on the doorstep, lifted it carefully inside, and shut the door.

Carrying the bag through to the kitchen, she placed it on the worktop, and stared at it, as if she could somehow determine its contents through the plastic. She couldn't. She teased the top open and peered in. And her eyes grew wide.

This called for something she hadn't done in a long time. She flicked on the TV and browsed the DVD shelves behind. Her mum organised the films by genre, because 'you didn't always know exactly what film you wanted to watch, but you always knew what kind of film you felt like'. And Leanne knew exactly what she felt like. Trashy romcoms. Something that required no effort on her part.

As the film started up, she grabbed the bag from the kitchen, and a spoon from the drawer, and settled herself on the couch, with her legs curled underneath her.

She couldn't remember when she last had ice cream or chocolate, but she was certain of one thing: it had never, ever, tasted so good.

13

Leanne woke to the sound of rain. It thundered against the ground outside, and spat against her bedroom window, drowning out any other sounds. Not that there were ever any other sounds to hear.

She sat up and rubbed her eyes. Then she stopped, and listened. But she couldn't hear anything past the rain.

Something was amiss. She could feel it. It felt like someone was in the house.

Sliding carefully out of bed, she crept out onto the landing and leaned over the banister. The hall was empty, and the front door was shut. There were no signs of an intruder, apart from the churning of Leanne's gut.

Years of creeping down to the fridge in the middle of the night, or to retrieve her phone that her mum had banned her from having in her bedroom meant that she knew every creak and squeak on the stairs, and she deftly avoided them.

She rounded the end of the banister into the hall and took a deep breath before peering into the living room.

Whatever she had expected, it wasn't this. The TV was on—perhaps she'd left it on last night—and showing nothing but static. Sat in front of it, cross-legged on the floor, her head blocking part of the screen, was a young girl.

"Hello?" Leanne ventured in barely more than a whisper. The girl didn't respond. "Hello?" Louder this time. Nothing. Leanne crept further into the room, trying to shake the paranoia from her head. She'd watched far too many horror films, and her head cycled through all manner of terrifying possibilities.

She drew almost level with the girl. "Hello?" She didn't even flinch. As Leanne came around the front of the girl, her heart raced at the images flicking through her mind; a girl with no eyes, no face, huge teeth, a huge mouth for a face, a cyborg, a zombie. She squeezed her eyes shut for a moment.

The girl was none of those things. She looked completely normal. Leanne sighed and crouched down.

"Can I help you?" she asked.

The girl's focus didn't waver from the TV.

"How did you get in here?" Leanne noted that her hair and clothes were dry. She hadn't come in to shelter from the rain. "What's your name? Are you lost?"

The girl's eyes didn't even flicker in her direction. It was as if she couldn't see or hear Leanne at all.

"Can I get you something to eat? I have chocolate."

Nothing. Leanne straightened up, unsure of what to do next. She lifted the girl's arm, and the girl snatched it back. She wasn't completely zombified. It wasn't some kind of weird coma. Nor was she merely an apparition conjured up by extreme loneliness.

Leanne sighed. "You really need to leave. You shouldn't be here." She didn't even expect a response.

Glancing around, she noticed the TV remote on the floor. She picked it up and turned the TV off.

For a moment, nothing happened. The girl didn't vanish, or get up and leave, or snap out of her trance. She just stared at the blank screen.

Then her focus flicked up to Leanne's face. She made a noise like a growl, guttural, and from deep inside her. The growl rose to an inhuman wail and she flung herself at Leanne, biting, scratching. The impact knocked Leanne to the floor, and the remote flew from her hand. It was like fighting off a wild animal, and Leanne folded an arm over her face. Nails and teeth tore at her clothes and any skin they could find. With her other arm, Leanne scrabbled for the remote. She twisted her head around and felt her cheek burn as the girl's nails dragged down it. Her fingers found the edge of the remote, and pulled it closer. She grabbed it, her thumb instinctively finding the standby button and pressing it hard.

She heard the slight ping as the screen illuminated, and in the same moment, the girl rolled off her and resumed her sentry in front of the static.

"Jesus," breathed Leanne, slowly pushing herself to her feet. She retreated into the hallway, keeping her eyes fixed on the back of the girl's head. She reached out for the banister, and ran up the stairs.

In the bathroom, she inspected her face and arms. She was covered in scratches and bite marks. Three bloody gouges ran down her cheek.

"That kid better not have rabies or anything," she muttered as she looked through the bathroom cabinet for antiseptic cream. "What a psycho."

Covered in paste, Leanne sank to the bathroom floor and leant back against the cold side of the bath. She wrapped her arms around herself and wished, with everything she had, that her parents would choose this moment to come back home.

14

Leanne raised her hand for the third time, finally managing to actually knock on Mr Hendricks' door. The spray paint was still as she'd left it; she hadn't cleaned enough of it off to conceal what it said.

She waited, pulling her hood further over her head, and hunching her shoulders against the rain. She knocked again, louder this time, more desperately. After a while, the door opened.

Mr Hendricks looked older. Tired. His shoulders seemed to have bowed under the weight of his head, and his face was dark, shadowed, his cheeks hollow. But at least he was still alive. At least he hadn't given up on everything.

"What do you want, Leanne?" he asked with a tone that clearly didn't want to know the answer.

Leanne took a deep breath. "I'm sorry to disturb you, but I really need your help. I just didn't know who else to ask. Please."

They stood in the doorway and looked at the girl.

"Where did she come from?" Mr Hendricks asked.

"I have no idea. All of the doors and windows were still locked. She wasn't wet from the rain, either. It's like she just materialised here. Or crawled out of the TV, or something."

Mr Hendricks walked around to the front of the girl and looked at her. Leanne remained in the doorway.

"And she did that to you?"

Leanne nodded, her fingers lifting towards her throbbing face. "As soon as I turned the TV off she went wild. It seems to keep her calm."

Mr Hendricks peered at the snow on the screen. "Or sedate her. Hypnotise her, perhaps."

"I'm just so scared of another blackout."

Mr Hendricks looks up at her. "Geez, I hadn't even thought of that." He frowned, thinking hard for a moment. "What if I just carry her outside and we lock the door?"

"And what if she gets back in? We don't know how she got in here in the first place."

He nodded slowly. "Like she just materialised..." he mumbled. "Maybe," he walked back to her, "she appeared just like people disappeared. What if this is how they're going to return? Just to show up as inexplicably as they went."

"But wouldn't she reappear where she

disappeared? Why here?"

Mr Hendricks shrugged. "Not necessarily. I mean, nothing about any of it makes any sense. We're nowhere close to understanding what happened to everyone, so we can't apply any kind of rules or logic to their return."

"I guess."

"What if your parents... My family... What if everyone's starting to come back?"

"Like this?" Leanne gestured towards the girl.

Mr Hendricks looked at the floor. "I don't know." He looked back up at her. "But we need to find out what we can. We need to make sense of this somehow. And to do that, we need to know who she is, where she came from. Why don't you take a photo of her and make some posters. We'll put them up all over town, and hopefully someone will recognise her."

"It will be nice to put up found posters instead of missing ones. Maybe it will give other people hope too. And I'll check at the church, see if I can find a missing poster with her on."

Leanne could feel a heat growing deep inside of her. It was good to have something new to focus on, something positive, something that could finally bring her some answers. She looked from Mr Hendricks down to the girl. Everything relied on her now; Leanne, Mr Hendricks, and the future of the entire world. And this child had no idea how important she was.

15

Leanne paused to touch the grainy faces of her parents. Next to it, she borrowed a pin from another poster and put up the one with the girl's face. She hadn't put her address on the posters, Mr Hendricks had insisted on that, but asked people to come to the church with any information they had instead. He said it was safer. We didn't know who might be interested in her.

She pushed open the glass doors and stepped into the cool, half-lit interior of the church. She looked up at the cavern of the vaulted ceiling above her. It would have once been filled with song, reverberating with the sound of faith, and belief, and hope. But now, it was just more empty space that people had abandoned.

"Hello?" Leanne called out, her voice impossibly loud. "Hello? Neil?"

"Hello, hello," he called back, stepping out of a doorway. He looked around and spotted her. "Leanne, hello, how nice to see you again." He swept down the aisle towards her, and took one of her hands into his as if they were old friends. "I'm glad you came back."

"I wasn't sure I'd find you here."

He waved a hand at her dismissively. "I don't really bother going home anymore. Even though it's the same as it always was, it somehow feels emptier there." He sighed. "Sometimes, the whole world feels empty." He released her hand and smiled. "Anyway, what can I do for you? Would you like a cuppa? Some toast?"

Leanne pulled a poster from her bag and passed it to him.

"I found a girl. Well, she kind of just appeared. Something's not right with her and, well, we think she might have come back. You know, from wherever people disappeared to."

Neil's eyes widened and he reached out to steady himself against a pew.

"You know what this means?" he whispered.

Leanne nodded. "I'm excited and terrified all at once. We want to find out who she is. I hope you don't mind, but I put for people to come here with any information about her. I didn't want to put my address on it."

Neil shook his head. "No, no, that's fine." He chewed his lip as he stared at the girl's photo.

"Do you recognise her?"

"No, I'm sorry. Have you checked the posters?"

"Not yet, but I was going to. Just in case."

Neil looked back at her picture. "This is big, Leanne."

"I know. And I don't even have anyone to tell. The police station has been shut up for almost a year, and there's no council, no authorities. And I'm certainly not going to go to The Arcane about it."

Neil nodded slowly. "Yes, yes. We need to find out who she is, return her home. How many of these posters do you have?"

"Not many. I just printed them off at home."

"We have a photocopier here, I guess it still works. If it does, I'll run off a few hundred and we can post them through letterboxes. We need to find out who this girl is. You realise how important she is, right? What's she said? What's she told you about where she's been?"

"She... um... doesn't really speak. It's like she doesn't even know I'm there."

"She's probably in shock."

"I think it might be more than that. It's like she's had a lobotomy."

"Right then. Let's check the foyer."

Leanne looked at missing posters until she could barely recognise a face as a face anymore, until the words became nonsense. Most of them were too faded to properly see anyway.

She dropped onto the bench. "I guess she's not here."

"Not that we can see. But don't give up, this little

girl belongs somewhere. Someone's missing her."

Leanne slipped her phone out of her pocket and looked at it. "If only we had the internet to help us."

"You've got a signal," Neil said, peering over her shoulder.

"Oh, yeah, I've had it for a couple of hours actually. But it's still not working."

Neil pulled his own phone from his pocket. "Habit," he explained. "I've got signal too." He selected a contact and lifted the phone to his ear. He shrugged. "Nothing. But, that's the longest we've ever had signal, right? It usually disappears after a couple of minutes."

"I guess." Leanne looked down at her shoes. "Why do you think she turned up in my house? Why me?"

"We'll probably never know. Perhaps it was random, perhaps it was by design."

"That I was chosen? Why would someone choose me?"

"Why not?"

Leanne shrugged. "I'm nothing special."

"In a world devoid of hope, you're actually very special." He sighed. "In a way, you're lucky that you're going through this as a child. You can bask in blind hope, it's almost expected of you. As an adult, corrupted by the world's cynicism, it's hard to push past the desire to apply reason and logic. But, there is no reason and logic to this." He sighed again. "Do you remember when, officially, the billionth person was reported missing?"

Leanne nodded.

"The media went crazy. The world went crazy. That was when everything started to unravel. Of course, the actual billionth person would have gone missing a long time before that."

"I guess so," Leanne said. "People who weren't reported missing."

"Right. Not every government was counting. But then, you also have the people that no one noticed were missing."

"That's really sad."

Neil nodded. "I always wonder, if I'd disappeared, how long it would have taken anyone to notice."

"But surely your friends here..."

"I doubt it. Besides, so many people were leaving the town by then." He shrugged and nodded his head towards the church. "Come here, I'll show you."

Leanne stood up and crossed the foyer to stand by him. They both looked into the church.

"I always sat in the same place." He pointed to a pew near the back. "No one ever sat with me. I was nearly always the first one here, but as everyone filed past, no one ever stopped to say hello or ask how my week had been. I always stayed after church for coffee, but it was nothing more than polite, obligatory small talk. I doubt most of them even knew my name."

"But you're the one keeping the church going. I assumed you must have been, I don't know, like a caretaker or something."

Neil shook his head. "I'm doing this mostly for myself, for my own selfish reasons. In the early days, lots of people came. I held their hands and led them in prayer. I made them hot drinks. I offered them words of comfort. And they knew my name." He snorted. "It took the entire world falling apart for anyone to finally learn my name."

"Well, I know your name, and I'm glad you didn't disappear."

He patted her shoulder. "Thank you. You're the only one who comes here anymore. I guess even the church can't offer hope anymore."

Leanne looked at the posters that flickered around them like a forest canopy. There was something hauntingly beautiful about it, like being in a paper cocoon.

"Do you still find hope here?" she asked Neil.

"I don't even know what hope is anymore."

"Don't say that. This girl is hope, surely."

He shook his head quickly, as if trying to dispel his anguish. "You're right, she is."

"Only, she's not quite come back the same. Not that I knew her before, of course, but she's... she's kind of like a zombie." Leanne whispered the word.

"What do you mean?"

"Like she's not quite on the same planet anymore. Or like she's..." Leanne chewed her lip, trying to think of a less weighted way to explain the situation. She couldn't. "It's like she's possessed, or had her soul stolen, or something. Is possession a real thing?"

"Over the centuries, a lot of different afflictions have been mistaken for possession or witchcraft. Epilepsy, autism, dementia. Shock even. We don't know what this girl's gone through, where she's been, and she's just a child. She may simply be in shock."

"Do you think she could have been in hell?" Leanne whispered.

Neil shrugged. "We might never know where they've been."

"Is it possible to recover from possession? I mean, I know about exorcism, but is it real? Does it really work?"

"It's not really practised anymore, certainly not in this country. What does that tell you?"

"I'm just... I'm scared that when my parents come back, they're going to be the same. And I'm scared that, in that case, I'd rather not have them back at all."

16

Leanne crouched down in front of the girl and inspected her face. She looked completely normal; there was no deadness in her eyes, just a vague dreaminess. They weren't sunken, or underlined with dark shadows. Her skin was smooth, her cheeks slightly rosy. Her head wasn't spinning around, and she wasn't spewing pea soup either. Definitely not a demonic possession.

Leanne looked at the snow on the TV. She relaxed her eyes, tried to see through the screen. She searched the snow for hidden messages.

She waved her hand in front of the girl's face. Nothing.

"What can you see that I can't?" she asked. "What can you hear?" She sighed and straightened up. "Do you want anything to eat?"

Leanne walked through to the kitchen and set

about making herself a sandwich. She watched the girl the whole time. It didn't make any sense.

She looked at her schoolwork spread across the table. She didn't know if she had the focus to sit and study; feeling restless, unsettled, unable to relax with a stranger in the house. But maybe she could absorb something.

Grabbing her phone, she leant against the toaster, and scrolled through the videos her teacher had sent her. It didn't matter which she chose, she was only using it for company.

She set it playing and turned to look out of the kitchen window. The clouds sat low and heavy in the sky, and a breeze played with the fallen leaves. Summer had finally left them to the care of autumn. She pushed the last bite of her sandwich into her mouth and turned back around.

The girl was standing by the dining table. Her head was cocked to one side. She was listening.

Leanne stepped forward and turned her phone around so that the girl could see it. She lifted it above her head, and watched as the girl's eyes followed it.

"You can hear this?" Leanne said.

The girl didn't respond, but continued to stare at the phone.

Leanne pressed pause. The girl blinked twice, turned, and returned to the TV. Leanne looked at her phone. "She could hear this," she whispered. She restarted the video, and watched as the girl's head turned, and she stood, and came back to watch the phone. Leanne paused the video once more, and watched as the girl returned to the TV. She followed her into the living room.

Opening her voice recorder app, Leanne spoke into it. "Can you hear this?" she said. She played the question back, and the girl looked up at her. "Can you hear this?" She played it again. The girl blinked twice. "Can you hear this?" The girl's mouth opened. "Can you hear this?"

A sound escaped the girl's throat, not quite a word. She swallowed and tried again. "Yes."

Leanne stared at her phone. "What's your name?" She recorded the question and played it back. Again, and then again.

Finally, the girl responded. "Casey," she said.

Leanne hammered on Mr Hendricks' door until her hand hurt. When he opened it, his face was flushed with panic.

"What is it?" he asked. "What's happened?"

"I found a way to talk to Casey."

"Who's Casey?"

"Oh, the girl." Leanne gestured wildly towards her house.

He stepped out of the door and pulled it shut behind him. "What did she say? Did she tell you where she came from? Where she's been? What's happened to her?"

"I haven't asked her anything yet, besides her name." Leanne had to jog across the lawn to keep up with Mr Hendricks.

"Why not?"

They stopped at Leanne's front door. She looked up at him. "Because I was scared to. I was scared of what the answer might be."

He took a breath and nodded. "Fair enough."

Leanne let them inside and they stood for a moment, looking at Casey.

"So, how do we do it?" Mr Hendricks asked.

Leanne handed him her phone. "You have to record what you want to say and then play it back to her."

"Really?"

"It seems that she can't hear voices that are right there next to her, but she can hear recorded voices. And understand them, too."

Mr Hendricks walked up to Casey. "Where have you been?" he said into the phone. He played it back and she looked up at him. "Where have you been?" He glanced up at Leanne with a frown. "What happened to you?" "Who took you?" "Where did they take you?" "What did they do to you?" His voice was becoming tight and strained, it's tone rising into a scream. "What do they want?" "Why have they done this?" He looked at Leanne again. "Why isn't she answering?"

"Because you're bombarding her, it takes time. I had to play each question several times before getting an answer. You have to be patient."

Mr Hendricks sighed. "Patient. Patient? This is the first chance we have to find out what's happened, why this has happened. This is the first link we have to our families. Don't you understand that?"

"Of course I do."

"And you're asking me to be patient? I've been patient for almost two years. Goddammit, I just want my damn family back."

"We all do. But we need to take this slowly. And gently. She's just a child."

"I know she's just a child," he snapped.

"Just like your girls," Leanne whispered. "If one of them had come back, you wouldn't want someone screaming a string of questions at them, would you?"

His shoulders slumped. "No."

"We can't hope for a miracle. She might not even know the answers."

"Hoping for a miracle is the only thing I have left." He turned away from her as he began to cry. It was what boys were trained to do.

Leanne crossed the room and eased the phone from his hand. "Let me try." She sat down in front of Casey. "Casey, where have you been?" she asked. Casey looked at her blankly. Leanne played the question again. And again.

"Asleep. Awake," Casey replied.

Mr Hendricks lifted his face from his hands. "She answered."

"You see? You just need to be patient."

"But what does she mean? Ask her again."

"Casey, where have you been?"

"Asleep. Awake."

Leanne looked at Mr Hendricks. "Perhaps we need to ask in a different way." She thought for a moment. "Casey, where have you been sleeping?"

"With the others. All of the others."

Mr Hendricks sucked in a quick breath. "Wherever they are, they're all together. Oh, thank God, they're all together."

The relief hit Leanne like a wave washing over her. She drowned in it, unable to draw a clean breath. She bit back tears and placed a hand flat against the floor to steady herself. "They're together," she whispered.

"Casey, where is everyone sleeping?"

"Hung. Like pictures. Plop, plop, plop, plop."

Leanne looked at Mr Hendricks. His face was pale, and she suspected hers matched.

"Maybe that's enough for now," he said, his voice shaking. "We're not getting much sense from this. How about we ask her simple things, like where she lived before."

Leanne nodded quickly. "Good idea." She was trying to ignore the images in her head, and she wasn't keen to add to them by probing Casey further. Safe, benign questioning would be better.

"Casey, where do you live?"

"15 White Willow Drive, Harroton."

"That's not far," said Mr Hendricks. "Just a couple of towns away. Probably less than an hour's drive."

"I wonder why she showed up here, instead of at home. Or where she went missing from."

"Perhaps, whoever took her, didn't care about where they returned her to. Like when we catch insects."

"Casey, who do you live there with?"

"My parents, Liam, and Buster."

"A brother and a pet?" Leanne said.

"I'd guess so."

"I wonder if they're all still there."

"I'm sure at least some of them will be. I can't remember ever hearing about a whole family disappearing. There was always someone left behind."

"Like a purposeful act of cruelty."

"Or the act of someone who doesn't understand family. We keep saying some*one*, but it could have been some*thing*."

They sat in silence for a moment, battling with their own thoughts and feelings.

"Like aliens?" Leanne whispered.

Mr Hendricks shrugged. "Or monsters. Or demons. There's so much in this world that we don't understand. Or don't even know about. There's depths of the oceans that we can't even get to. They're discovering new species every day. And space? As far as we know, it's endless. It's hugely unlikely that there's no other life out there."

"Do you think we should take her home?"

"Yes. Yes, I do. But how? It's a long way to walk."

"Do you have a car?"

"Yes, in the garage, but it hasn't even been started in more than a year. We'll never get it going now."

"If we could get it started, would you drive us to Harroton?"

Mr Hendricks shrugged. "I have nothing better to do. But what do we do about the TV, about her needing to watch it?"

"I wonder if an untuned radio would work. If it's the sound, rather than the static on the screen. And it's not like there's any stations to actually tune into these days."

17

Leanne looked at the expression on Mr Hendricks' face. The car looked fine to her. Dusty, but fine. But his face told her different.

He climbed inside and ran his hand along the dashboard. He glanced into the back, his daughters' car seats still strapped in. He looked back at Leanne through the murky windscreen.

"Here goes nothing," he said.

And nothing happened. Leanne listened hard, but the car made no sound at all.

"Well, I guess that really was nothing," Mr Hendricks said. He disappeared down behind the dashboard and the bonnet popped open with a clunk. "Let's have a look," he said, coming round to the front of the car. He propped the bonnet open and peered in at the engine.

"Do you know what you're looking at?" Leanne

stepped forward and surveyed the array of pipes, and shapes, and things she didn't recognise.

"Nope," he said. "Not really. It's definitely going to need a new battery, probably spark plugs, new filters, probably clean fuel which means draining the tank." He looked round at her. "It's a big job, and we need a lot of parts. There's no way I can do it alone."

Leanne sighed. "So that's it then."

Mr Hendricks slammed the bonnet shut. "It's not that bad, it's just like getting a full service. Kind of. But we'll need a mechanic."

"If we can find one. And then we'll have to pay them. What are we going to pay them with? I don't have any access to my parents' accounts."

"Money's pretty much worthless these days anyway. We'll have to barter with something they want."

"What do people consider valuable these days?"

"It doesn't matter what *people* consider valuable, it matters what the *mechanic* considers valuable. But, first we need to actually find one willing to barter, then we need to find out what they want, then we need to see if we can get it. Unless..." He jiggled his hands around. "Unless you want to ask Joel's people for help."

"No. We can do this by ourselves."

"Right, bartering it is then. I might be able to find a phone book somewhere—" he snorted, "remember them? My wife always hoarded them for some reason that I never quite understood."

"Lucky she did."

He nodded. "Of course, we'll have to actually go to all the garages, on foot, seeing as we have no phones now. That means it's going to take time. Do you think Casey will be ok left on her own?"

"As long as the TV stays on, she'll be fine.

18

Bleary-eyed, Leanne pulled the front door open. It was Mr Hendricks, and he was jiggling up and down like an excited child.

"It's barely even morning," she groaned.

"Some things are too important to wait around for your teenage body clock." He pushed past her and stopped at the living room door. "How is she?"

"No change. Let me go and get dressed."

When Leanne came back downstairs, Casey was looking up at Mr Hendricks. After a moment, her attention turned back to the TV.

"Are you ready?" Leanne asked.

"I've been ready for ages. Let's go."

Leanne grabbed her coat from the rack in the hall and pulled it on. "At least it's not raining."

"Hope you've got your walking shoes on." Mr

Hendricks walked on ahead like someone out of a cheery, upbeat musical. Arms swimming, striding forward. Leanne prayed that he wasn't going to burst into song.

She trailed behind, her shoulders hunched into a cringe. It was clear that he had pinned all of hopes onto the mission. Despite her warnings, he believed that this girl would somehow be the answer to getting his family back. She recognised that hope. It had also burnt inside her when Casey had first arrived. But as they walked, and found garage after garage either locked down tight, or ransacked of anything of any value, that hope was quickly dispersing into something much darker. Something that was far heavier to carry. She looked up at Mr Hendricks, his jaw set hard, and wondered how long they'd be able to avoid admitting that this was a lost cause.

"Right," said Mr Hendricks, breaking Leanne from her thoughts, "the next one should be along here somewhere." They walked a little farther before the forecourt opened on their right.

In the middle of the empty space was a plastic garden chair, and sitting in the chair was a man. He was facing the garage, his back towards them.

Mr Hendricks batted Leanne's arm excitedly and strode across the forecourt.

"Excuse me," he called out. "Excuse me."

The man slowly turned his head, looked Mr Hendricks up and down, and then returned his focus to the garage.

Mr Hendricks drew level with him. "Excuse me, are you open? We're looking for a mechanic."

The man sighed, his broad shoulders heaving up to his ears before dropping back down as if they were weighted with rocks. He shook his head.

"No. All the mechanics have gone." He lifted his hands, fanning out his fingers like popping bubbles. "Poof."

"They all disappeared?"

The man shrugged again. "They may as well have. Disappeared, left town, betrayed and abandoned me. What's the difference?"

"We really need some parts."

The man gestured towards the garage. "Take what you want, if there's anything left. I can't help you find what you need, though, I know nothing about cars." He wearily raised his eyes to Mr Hendricks' face. "I inherited this place from my father, he'd wanted me to follow him into the family business. I wish I had now. At least I'd have some skills that were actually useful. Not that it matters anymore anyway. Not that anything matters anymore."

Mr Hendricks looked back at Leanne and cocked his head towards the garage. "May as well take a look."

They ducked under the shutters and stood, waiting for their eyes to adjust to the gloom inside.

Leanne looked around with a heart that had sunk into her shoes.

"He wasn't joking about there not being anything

left." Mr Hendricks bent and picked up a washer from the floor. He held it out to Leanne. "Looks like this is about it."

She took it from him and slipped it into her pocket. "For luck," she said.

"It wasn't very lucky for that guy out there."

"It's still here, and anything that's still here is lucky." She turned away from the emptiness, from the toppled shelves, the discarded drawers, and looked up at the shadow board behind her. Somehow, this was the worst. The painted shapes of tools that were no longer there. Just the ghosts remaining.

"It's like Peter Pan," she whispered.

"The tools that didn't want to grow up."

Leanne shot Mr Hendricks a look. "It's sad," she said.

He nodded. "Let's get out of here. There's nothing here for us."

"Do you think the owner will be ok?"

"Is anyone ok?"

As they left, they wished him good luck, and he raised a half-hearted hand in reply.

"Do you think there's any hope of finding another garage open?" Leanne asked.

"I don't know.," Mr Hendricks replied. "I guess we'll just have to keep our fingers crossed and hope that the universe is on our side."

Leanne huffed. "I'm not sure the universe is on anyone's side."

"Still, we have to keep trying, for Casey's sake, and for her family's sake. And, maybe, if we return

Casey to where she belongs, the universe might actually owe us a favour."

"That would be nice." Leanne turned as she heard someone shouting behind them, her hand instinctively laying on Mr Hendricks' arm. She felt his muscles tense under her touch. He turned.

"Hey! Hey! Wait up!" The owner of the garage was running towards them, waving his arms madly above his head.

They stopped and waited for him to catch them up.

"I only just thought; one of my mechanics set up working from home after everything happened. He's basically employed by The Arcane now, taking care of all their mechanic jobs, he said it was a matter of survival. I haven't spoken to him for several months, but last time I did, he was still doing private jobs on the side. As long as the price was right, of course. I don't know if that's still the case, but it's always worth a try." He handed Mr Hendricks a scrap of paper. "You're not going to find a garage around that hasn't already been ransacked by either gangs or chancers. There might be other mechanics working from home, but I haven't heard of any. I mean, The Arcane want to protect their assets, so I'd be surprised if they let anyone set up in competition. Honestly," he shook his head, "you'd think they were the mob, not just a bunch of kids running round a shitty little town. They've obviously watched far too many movies."

"Thank you," Mr Hendricks said. "This is

definitely a better lead than following an old phone book."

They shook hands.

"Well," said the owner, "good luck to you."

"Thanks. You too."

Leanne waited for him to be out of earshot before she spoke. "Mr Hendricks, I'm not sure about this. If he's working for The Arcane—"

"This is the only chance we have. You heard what he said. We're not going to find any garages still open."

"But—"

"Do you want to get Casey home or not? This is the only way." He shrugged. "What have we got to lose?"

Leanne sighed and followed without further argument. She pushed the feeling of dread down into the depths of her stomach where it was easier to ignore. She'd gotten used to the feeling of it there, like she'd swallowed a stone.

When they reached the address on the slip of paper, they found several cars parked on the street, and yet more crammed onto the small drive. A young man was under the bonnet of one, shoulder-deep in its engine.

On the overgrown lawn beyond, a couple of other men were slouched on sun loungers. They stood up as Leanne and Mr Hendricks stepped onto the driveway. Leanne didn't take her eyes off them, every muscle in her body tensed and ready to run.

Mr Hendricks raised his hands. "We're just looking for a mechanic," he said loudly.

The mechanic straightened and approached them. He waved a hand at the other two men, and they resumed their positions on the sun loungers.

"How can I help?" the mechanic asked.

"I just need to get my car going. It's not been started in more than a year, and I tried the ignition and got absolutely nothing at all. I guess, new battery, spark plugs, filters, clean fuel."

The mechanic gave a low whistle. "That's not a simple job. If the engine's seized..." He cocked his head from side to side weighing things up. "I'd have to look at it before I can say whether I can get it going or not. And it's going to cost you. A job like that won't come cheap." He looked Mr Hendricks up and down. "I'm not sure you'll be able to afford it." He peered around Mr Hendricks at Leanne. He sidestepped for a better view, and looked her over with a gaze that felt like hands on her. "Then again..." he said.

Mr Hendricks stepped back in front of her. "Take a look at the car, and then we'll talk cost. I'll get whatever you want."

Leanne glanced over at the two men on the lawn and mustered up everything she had inside her. She rolled all of her feelings up inside her stomach like newspaper, and then she lit a match. She patted Mr Hendricks on the arm and, before she could talk herself out of it, marched across the grass towards them.

They looked up at her with a look of casual

amusement.

"Hey, I know you," she said to one of them, adopting as much of a flippant tone as she could manage.

"Do you?" The guy sat up and frowned at her.

"Yeah. You've brought us food a few times. I'm Joel's sister."

Recognition flooded his face and spread into a smile. "Oh yeah. I remember now." He nodded towards Mr Hendricks. "That your dad?"

"No, my neighbour. I'm just helping him out." She lowered her voice. "He lost his whole family."

He nodded. "Oh yeah, and you guys lost your folks."

"That's right. Can you help us out? He needs to get out of here, away from all the memories of them. He just can't take it anymore."

"I'm sure that we can," the other man said, sitting up. "Joel's a good'un. Works hard, does as he's told. He's loyal, and that's valuable."

"He's away at the moment."

"Yes, of course." He turned and called over to the mechanic. "Take the job. Whatever they need. No charge."

19

Over the next few days, Leanne talked often with Casey. It lessened her sense of unease, her growing fear that things were about to get a lot worse.

The more they talked, the easier it became. Casey needed fewer repetitions of the questions, she seemed to be more alert, and her answers were becoming more coherent. They talked about school, and books, and music, and movies, and the boys they liked. Safe topics. But a gulf still sat between them, and Leanne knew that she couldn't avoid it forever. It was as empty as it was deep, and she feared the fall into it. But she had to ask. She had to ask Casey where she'd been.

"Everyone is there together. Sleeping, but awake."

"In the same room?" Leanne played the recorded question back.

"It's not a room. It's just space."

"It's outdoors?"

"There is no indoors or outdoors. It's just space. It's everywhere and nowhere."

"You mean it's like space? Like where the stars are?"

"Purple sky. No sun, no moon, no stars. Just space. And people. Sleeping, but awake."

"Can the people talk to each other?"

"No one talks. They just think. They think straight into your head like it's just you doing the thinking."

Leanne sat back and breathed hard. "I don't understand," she muttered to herself. She looked back at Casey and spoke into her phone. "What do the people do?"

"They hang. In the air. In lines. Like pictures. They don't move, or eat, or drink. They breathe into tubes and their heartbeats click and click and click. Click, click, click, click. Millions of heartbeats."

Leanne gazed at the TV. Millions of heartbeats. Like static. She took a deep breath and lifted her phone back to her mouth. "Why did you come back, Casey? Why not anyone else?"

"They were finished with me. They took everything they wanted. Both of them."

"Both of them?"

"Them. And then them."

"What did they want with you?"

"They gave me something. Something to share with all of the others. Something to bring back."

Leanne's heart hammered as she recorded the next question. "What were you meant to bring back?"

"I don't know the word. I don't know what it means."

"Can you remember how to say it? What it sounded like?"

"Of course." She nodded towards the TV. "They keep saying it to me."

Leanne looked at the screen and listened. The blood pounding through her ears seemed to drown out every other sound in the world. She doubted she'd have heard a bomb going off. She shook her head to try and clear it.

"What's the word, Casey?"

"Termination."

20

Leanne opened the front door and Mr Hendricks was standing outside, a wide grin on his face.

"The car's finally ready. Kris got it started this morning."

"Oh. Right."

Mr Hendricks frowned at her. "Not more excited?"

Leanne kneaded the back of her neck. "I just didn't sleep too well, I'm tired. Ignore me. That's great news."

Mr Hendricks gestured to where the car was parked on the street, its engine running. The sound was so odd, so alien. So intrusive. Leanne could hardly believe she had heard it every day of her life, and it had become nothing but background noise. It felt like her skull was rattling from the vibrations.

"I don't want to turn it off," he said. "Just in case

we can't get it going again. Are you ready?"

"Erm..." Leanne looked around her. "I was expecting a little bit more notice. I mean, what should I take? How long are we going to be gone?"

"Well, we can be there in less than an hour, and then, however long we're at Casey's house, chatting with her parents, finding out what we can. Then back here. We may well be back by lunchtime."

Leanne backed up into the house and looked at Casey. "We need to get her to the car. Without her... y'know."

Mr Hendricks looked at Casey and chewed his bottom lip. "Maybe we just bundle her into a blanket and make a run for it. It's not that far to the car."

"I think that's too dangerous." She touched the scabs that lined her cheek. "She's really vicious, and what if she got away from us and ran off somewhere?"

He frowned and nodded. "Have you got a portable radio?"

"I'm not sure I'd even know what one looked like."

Mr Hendricks rolled his eyes. "Kids. I think we might have one in the attic, or the basement, or somewhere. Let me go look. Keep an eye on the car."

Leanne stood in the open doorway and looked at the vehicle. She didn't know what Mr Hendricks expected her to do if someone did jump into it and drive off. She looked up and down the street. It was empty, as always.

Across the road, a movement caught her eye; a

curtain falling back into place. Someone was watching. But she knew the house, and Mrs Lowstock was elderly and harmless. Her grandson, however, ran with The Arcane. Joel had told her that. They already knew about the car, of course, but busybodies had a way of complicating things, and the fewer people who knew their business, the safer they were.

Leanne looked over at Mr Hendricks' house. His front door stood open. She looked back at Mrs Lowstock's front window. Everything was still. She didn't trust that though; the woman had always been a curtain twitcher. She'd approached her mum in the street once, offering some kind of parenting advice. It hadn't been received very well, and Leanne and Joel had been taught to be suspicious of those curtains.

She looked up and down the empty street again. And now she was suspicious of all the windows. They watched her. She looked down at the car, its exhaust shaking and dripping, like the mouthpiece of some kind of monster. She looked away.

She jumped as her pocket buzzed; her phone vibrating. The tinny sound of music followed. She'd forgotten her ringtone; some song her and her friends had been mad over forever ago. She pulled it out of her pocket and it vibrated in her hand, the sensation terrifyingly alien. Joel's name showed on the screen.

"Hello?" The connection crackled and fizzed, but somewhere under it all, she could hear Joel's voice. Tears ran down her cheeks. "Hello? Joel? I can barely hear you."

Through the static, she distinguished two things: "told you they were looking after us" and "I'll be home soon."

"How soon?" she asked, but the call had already ended. She stared at her phone in her hand.

"Here we go," Mr Hendricks hurried across to her, waving a portable radio above his head. "I knew we had one somewhere. I swear, my wife never throws anything out."

"It's helped us out a lot," Leanne muttered.

"What's happened?"

She rubbed her wet cheeks. "Joel just called."

"Called? You mean on the phone?"

Leanne laughed. "It's the first time I've spoken on a phone in more than a year. How crazy is that?"

Mr Hendricks laughed along with her.

"The signal was terrible, I could barely hear what he was saying. But it was signal. A phone call."

"Maybe things are starting to turn around."

Leanne looked back at her phone. "Maybe."

"Oh, I found this too." He held a map out to her, the thick bundle neatly folded. "A local map, it's got Harroton in it, all the streets." He grinned. "My wife bought it for me a couple of years ago, when I talked about starting cycling. Of course, it never happened. It's awful the things we keep putting off, keep finding excuses not to do, isn't it? This was meant to be something we were going to do together, but it's too late now. Still, it's going to be a huge help to us today." He laughed. "Funny how life turns out."

"Yeah, your wife's hoarding keeps helping us

out."

Mr Hendricks handed her the map. "Here. You can be my navigator. When I think of all the times I told her to get rid of it all, that it was of no use to anyone. Maybe she knew something we didn't."

"Maybe."

He waved the radio at her. "Let's give this a try then, shall we?"

They stepped inside, and Leanne slipped the map into her bag slumped at the bottom of the stairs. She turned and joined Mr Hendricks, looking at Casey. He turned the radio on and it hissed with static.

He looked at Leanne. "Ready?"

She retrieved the TV remote and backed up to the doorway.

"Stand behind me," Mr Hendricks said.

Leanne flicked the TV off. For a moment, Casey remained still, staring at the blank screen. Slowly, her head turned, and she pivoted her body around to face them. She looked at the radio.

"So far, so good," Mr Hendricks whispered.

They backed up to the front door and, after a moment, Casey appeared in the hallway. They stepped outside and Mr Hendricks carried the radio down the path. Casey followed. Mr Hendricks smiled at Leanne.

"It worked," he said quietly.

Leanne grabbed her bag and locked the front door behind them, skipping ahead to open the back door of the car. She helped Casey inside, and pulled the seatbelt across her. The interior of the car seemed so cramped, so enclosed, but it felt oddly exposed too, with the panorama of glass around them. She couldn't imagine travelling at sixty miles per hour in, essentially, a tin can with windows.

She pulled her head out of the car and stepped back. Mr Hendricks was already in the driving seat, peering expectantly through the passenger side window.

She opened the door.

"Are you getting in?" he asked.

Leanne swallowed back the lump of panic that rose in her throat and climbed into the seat. She closed the door and wondered if this was what astronauts felt like on their first flight. If only she had a helmet to hide inside.

"Sorry," she muttered. "It's just been a long time since I was in a car."

"I get that. I only hope I can remember how to drive." He flashed her a smile, and she hoped that he was joking. He flicked on the car radio, and gestured to the portable one gripped in Leanne's hands. "You should turn that off. Save the battery."

"Oh yeah." She switched it off and laid it in her lap.

"Here we go." With a jolt, they pulled away from the curb and set off.

As the world rushed towards the windscreen, and flew past them on either side, Leanne gripped the edge of her seat. She couldn't remember the last time she'd been in a car; probably her mum ferrying her somewhere, to a friend's house, to the library, or out shopping for the day. Lifts that she simply expected, and never said thank you for.

"Have you managed to talk to Casey any more?" Mr Hendricks asked.

"Not really."

"You haven't managed to find out anything about where she's been then?"

"No," Leanne lied. She just couldn't bring herself to say the words out loud. Not for her own sake, but also for the sake of Mr Hendricks. He had two young daughters there, as well as his wife. "Just more stuff about before she disappeared. Nothing of use."

"We'll explain to her parents how to speak to her, and maybe we can find some way to keep in touch with them, in case Casey does say something."

"I doubt they'll get anything. After all, she is just a child. A scared, confused child. We shouldn't expect anything. Besides, wherever she's been, she might have been unconscious the whole time. We might never get any answers. We might never know the truth, and I guess we just have to accept that."

Mr Hendricks glanced at her. "What happened to my little beacon of hope?"

Leanne winced.

"We'll ask her parents when she went missing. Maybe people are coming back in the same order they went. We could work out a timeline, work out when our families might turn up again."

"But how will we know where they'll return? Casey randomly turned up here. What if they come back on the other side of the world?"

They sat in silence for a while.

"We'll just have to hope," Mr Hendricks finally said. "We'll talk to her parents, find out what we can, and go from there."

21

Mr Hendricks squinted through the windscreen, leaning forwards so that his chest almost touched the steering wheel. "What's that?"

Leanne peered too, frowning to make sense of the unfamiliar shapes that covered the road ahead.

Mr Hendricks sat back. "It's some kind of roadblock. That's all we need." He slowed the car to a stop.

"It'll be The Arcane, keeping control of the supply routes."

"Did you know about this?"

"No, I honestly didn't. Joel's never mentioned it."

Mr Hendricks glanced back at Casey. "That means there'll be questions. They can't know who she is, God only knows what they'll do with her."

"Is there a way around? Some quiet back street or country lane they won't have blocked off?"

"Not without a big detour, and I don't know if we have enough petrol. They weren't exactly generous with that."

Leanne glared at the roadblock ahead. "We'll just have to go for it. After all, we have nothing to hide; just a dad and his two daughters leaving town after giving up hope of their mum ever coming back. They'll soon realise we're of no interest to them."

"What if they recognise you?"

Leanne waved a hand at him dismissively. "That's so unlikely. I've only ever met a couple of them, the chances of one of them being here is pretty low."

"Ok then. Here goes nothing." He rolled the car onwards to the roadblock.

The indistinguishable shapes across the road were nothing more than a line of shopping trolleys chained together, acting as a makeshift rolling gate. A garden shed had been erected next to them, and it was from here that a young lad, barely older than Leanne herself, swaggered out. With his thumbs tucked into his belt, he sauntered over to the car, making a great show of looking it over as if checking its road-worthiness. He approached the driver's window and tapped on the glass.

Mr Hendricks shot Leanne a tired look and lowered the window. Leanne stifled a giggle.

"Can you switch your engine off?" the boy said.

Mr Hendricks glanced at the radio, still spewing out static. "Actually, it took so much work to get it started, I'd rather not. In case I can't get it going again."

"Whatever." The boy was giving the nonchalant air of authority a real go. Leanne wondered which TV character he'd based himself on for the role. "These your girls?"

"My daughters, yes."

"Planning on leaving town?"

"Yes."

The guy shifted his weight, hopefully realising that he wasn't getting very far.

"Why?"

Mr Hendricks sighed. "Because we've waited for their mum to come back for long enough. It's time for a fresh start, to get away from all the memories."

"Lost your wife, did you?"

Mr Hendricks sighed again. "Yes."

Leanne looked at his profile, hoping he'd be able to maintain their cover story. If he broke down talking about his wife, he might forget what he was supposed to say. She wanted to touch his arm, to remind him to stay strong, to show him he wasn't alone. She was relying on him, and she wanted him to have someone to rely on in return.

"When did that happen?"

"21 months ago. And 12 days. Would you like the hours as well, because I am counting them."

The guy shifted again, glancing around him as if looking for backup. There was none. Just a kid with a job far beyond his age.

"That won't be necessary. Where are you headed?"

"Not really sure. I have an aunt in Scotland, but I don't have enough petrol to get there, if she's even still there. So, I guess we'll drive until we run out of fuel and just see where we end up."

"That seems a bit risky with two girls."

Mr Hendricks shrugged. "Perhaps. But I'm sure that you can relate to doing something without any real idea of how it'll pan out."

The guy frowned. "What is that noise?"

"The radio."

"There is no radio anymore."

Mr Hendricks hooked his thumb towards Casey. "My daughter likes the white noise. It's comforting. Like how people play it for babies to get them to sleep, you know?"

"Well, it's doing my head in." He leaned in through the window, his skinny arm reaching out and flicking the radio off.

Leanne switched the portable radio back on and tossed it behind her seat into the footwell beyond.

The boy shot her a look, but recoiled from inside the car.

"What was your wife's name?"

"Sarah."

"What did she do?"

"She worked in payroll four days a week, and volunteered in a charity shop on the fifth."

"How did she disappear?"

"She went into the kitchen to make me a drink. Would you like to hear about all the sleepless nights I've had since, wishing that I had offered to put the kettle on? That I hadn't been so engrossed in some pointless documentary that I honestly can't even remember what it was about anymore? That I'd just gone and made the damned drinks myself. Would you like to question me about that?"

The boy retreated from the car, his hands plunged deep into his pockets.

"Yeah, well, I'm expecting a delivery, and I can't have this rust bucket blocking the road." He crossed to the line of trolleys and pulled them back out of the way. He waved them through.

As they left Chatstone, Mr Hendricks looked at Leanne. "He seemed very adept at moving that long line of trolleys. I wonder if that was what he used to do. Maybe that's why they posted him there. His trolley-moving abilities. Who would've known it looked so good on his CV, eh?"

"Was that stuff true? What you said about your wife?"

Mr Hendricks stared at the road ahead. "Give a punk kid like that a tiny bit of authority and he suddenly thinks he's lord and master instead of the little shitbrick he's been all of his life."

22

The road between Chatstone and Harroton was a straight stretch of dual carriageway, and they saw no other cars, no signs of life, bar a few cows grazing on the verge.

As Mr Hendricks took the car down the slip road, and cornered the roundabout, they saw Harroton ahead. It began with a retail park, a single vehicle abandoned in the expanse of car parks. Then office blocks and industrial buildings, their broken windows full of ragged teeth and darkness. Forklift trucks stood outside, forgotten, lorries half-filled and then ransacked.

"Have you noticed the graffiti?" Leanne asked.

Mr Hendricks slowed the car and peered through the windscreen. "It's everywhere. What am I meant to be looking for in particular?"

"The writing. I've seen the same word repeated

over and over." She pointed. "There. 'Poisonmarch'. What do you suppose it means?"

Mr Hendricks shrugged. "It's probably the gang that's in charge here. Just marking their territory. Like dogs."

"Maybe. Seems excessive."

"A lot of people think that talking loudly makes them right. This is just an equivalent form of that."

Leanne nodded, but something in her gut didn't agree. The tagging was almost obsessive, like madness. Coupled with how desolate Harroton seemed, how truly devoid of life, how forsaken; Leanne couldn't ignore the churning of her stomach or the clamminess of her hands. Something in Harroton was very, very wrong.

"Get the map," Mr Hendricks said. "Let's see where we're going."

She tugged it from her bag, and found that he'd already folded it with Harroton clearly displayed. The whole thing opened out like a vast picnic blanket, full of creases that peaked and troughed like mountains and valleys, creases that a person could get lost in.

She looked down at the tangle of roads and found his pen marks. One to show where they'd be coming into Harroton, and another pinpointing White Willow Drive. They navigated the town easily enough, with no need to follow one-way systems or stop at red lights. Which was lucky, considering every set of lights they came across were on red. Leanne pushed away the thought that it was the universe trying to warn them to turn back.

The shops they passed had been looted, their security shutters buckled, their windows smashed. The houses they passed were in a similar state, with much of their furniture broken on the street outside, as if someone had picked them up and tipped out their contents like a box of toys.

White Willow Drive was a sweeping curve populated with large, semi-detached houses. Any hope of finding it in a better state than the rest of the town faded instantly. The doors stood ajar, some at jaunty angles as they clung desperately to a single hinge. The windows were smashed, the furniture scattered across the lawns and driveways.

Leanne turned round to Casey. Her attention had shifted from staring at the radio by her feet, to gazing out of the window. As Mr Hendricks stopped the car outside her house, she unbuckled herself and slid across the back seat.

Leanne nudged Mr Hendricks' arm, and they both watched her with fascination.

She stared out of the window, the glass fogging under her quickening breath. "Mum?" she whispered. "Dad?" She jostled the door handle.

"Child lock," Mr Hendricks muttered. He jumped out and opened the door for her.

She tumbled out of the car and staggered up the path, running blindly towards the house, and disappearing through the open front door.

"She woke up," Leanne said, grabbing her bag and climbing out of the car.

"It must have been the familiarity of home."

"So perhaps she wasn't in an induced trance at all. Maybe it was just shock and trauma."

"We should check that she's ok. She's obviously not going to find her family at home."

Casey was in the living room, staring up at the walls. Floor to ceiling, covering every inch, the word 'Poisonmarch' was written over and over.

"Do you still think this is just the local gang?" Leanne asked.

"Look," Mr Hendricks pointed at a mattress that had been leant against the front window. "It's like someone tried to hide here. Or barricade themselves in."

"What were they hiding from?"

Mr Hendricks turned around, dragging his fingers back through his hair. "What happened here?"

"I know what this means," Casey said quietly. She turned to look at Leanne. "I know what this word means."

"What does it mean, Casey?" Mr Hendricks asked.

Casey kept her focus on Leanne. "This is what they're doing. This is what they call it, all of this—" she flapped her arms around "—everything they've done, taking people. They call it the Poisonmarch."

"Who's 'they'?" Mr Hendricks looked from Leanne to Casey, and back again.

Leanne sighed. "I didn't tell you before, when you asked. You asked if Casey had told me anything, and I lied, I said she hadn't. But she had. She's told me a lot. But it really scared me and... with your family...

I just couldn't bring myself to tell you."

He stepped towards her. "Tell me what?"

Casey moved between them. "The things that took us all, they're keeping everyone plugged into these machines, like they're monitoring them. They want us all to bring something back with us. And they want—" she looked at Leanne. "What was that word again?"

Leanne stared at the carpet beneath her feet. More specifically, she stared at a small brown stain. "Termination," she said quietly.

"What?" Even in that single word, she could hear the shake in his voice. She looked up at him. His face was drained of colour, and his eyes were wide and bulging. He barely even looked like himself. He took another step towards her. "And you weren't going to tell me?"

"Because I was scared—"

"My girls were taken!" he screamed at her. "And you're telling me that they're going to be bringing something back? Something to terminate us all? They're tiny. They're just tiny, little girls." He grabbed Casey by the shoulders. "Have you got it? Have you already brought back this thing?" He started to shake her, snapping her head back and forth.

"I don't know!" she cried out. "I don't know what they put into me!"

"Why you? Why did you come back? Why only you?"

"I don't know!"

"Mr Hendricks, please." Leanne grabbed hold of

his arm, but he flung her back.

"Were you ever going to tell me?" he growled.

"I didn't know how you'd react. You seem so fragile half of the time, like you're barely holding it together..."

"I lost everyone I loved, of course I'm barely holding it together. What if my girls are out there somewhere, trying to find a way home?"

"I'm sorry."

He stared at her with a gaze like a shard of pure hatred. It cut right through her.

"I'm sorry," she said again.

"I'll bet you are."

Leanne and Casey followed him to the front door and watched as he climbed into the car and drove away.

Leanne sat down on the doorstep and dropped her head into her hands. "What was I thinking? Of course I should have told him."

"He would have freaked out all the same," Casey said.

"But at least we wouldn't be stuck miles from home."

Casey sighed and sat down next to her. "Well, I'm home already, and it isn't any comfort."

Leanne looked up at her and managed a smile. "I guess so."

"Do you think he'll come back? Once he's calmed down a bit?"

Leanne shrugged.

"Don't blame yourself." Casey patted her on the

shoulder. "He did go a bit psycho. Not telling him was probably a good call."

"Are you alright? He shook you pretty hard."

Casey grinned. "I was kidnapped by monsters. Do you really think a bit of a shake is going to hurt me?"

Leanne laughed down her nose. "I guess not." She rubbed at her face and sat upright. "Let's at least do something useful. Maybe we can find some sort of clue about what happened to your family, or something that will tell us more about what happened here." She shrugged. "You never know."

She pushed herself to her feet, and they went back inside.

The kitchen had been emptied of food, crockery, cutlery, even the toaster and kettle had been taken. The microwave was smashed to pieces in the utility room. There were heavy pieces of furniture pushed up against the back door. The rest of the house had suffered a similar fate; anything that might be worth anything, and anything that might be useful, had already been taken. The rest had been broken and discarded.

Leanne found Casey in one of the bedrooms. Judging by the décor, this had been her room. She was staring at the space the bed had once occupied, the carpet marked with squares where the feet had pressed in. Just like the shadow board at the garage.

Leanne touched her shoulder, and she jumped.

"Are you ok?" Leanne asked.

Casey nodded. "I guess. It's just... this doesn't feel

like my room anymore. It doesn't feel like home. So much has happened, it feels like something I did in another life, or a different version of me. Does that make sense?"

"A lot has happened. Do you feel changed by it?"

Casey frowned. After a moment, she said "Me, but not me."

"I guess I've only really thought about what everyone who was left behind has been going through. Thought that we were the only ones suffering. I never really thought about what everyone who disappeared might be feeling. As if all of your lives just kind of stopped. Like you were all put on pause."

Casey wandered over to the window and looked out at the garden below. "It did feel a little bit like that. I was aware of hanging there, breathing, but it was only a slight awareness. Like when you're halfway between asleep and awake, and you can still see your dream as well as hearing noises in the real world."

"And they all kind of mix in together," Leanne added.

"Right." Casey sighed deeply. "Oh my God, the spires!" she exclaimed, slamming her hand against the window.

"What's up?"

Casey turned and looked at her excitedly, her finger jabbing towards the view outside. "The spires. I forgot. There's three churches in Harroton that form a perfect triangle. That's why they came here. They drew their power from it."

"From the spires?"

"From the triangle."

"Pass me the map." Casey held out her hand.

Looking down, Leanne realised it was still clutched in her grip. She'd forgotten she was carrying it. She handed it over, and they bent their heads together.

"Look," said Casey. "There, there, and there." She pointed to three church symbols. "A perfect triangle."

Leanne stared at them. "I wonder if Chatstone's the same."

Kneeling, she unfolded the map across the floor until Chatstone was revealed. She searched the maze of streets, but found nothing.

"It can't be triangles. Chatstone doesn't have one."

Casey knelt next to her and frowned, her eyes flicking back and forth.

"There." She pointed to a church icon. "And what's that?"

Leanne leaned closer. "The town hall."

"And that?" Casey pointed again.

"Um... my school. But they're not spires." Leanne leaned back. "But the school does have a radio mast. And the town hall has a flagpole. Could they work?"

Casey shrugged. "I guess so. They're metal, and they're sticking up."

"Chances are, you'd be able to find a triangle like this in every town in the UK then. I mean, how big do the, um, conductors, I guess, need to be? Almost every house still has a TV aerial."

The sound of a car engine outside rattled through the house. The rumble of it so unexpected, so out of place, yet, two years ago, they wouldn't have even noticed it.

"Mr Hendricks," Leanne said. She haphazardly folded the map and forced the untidy bundle into her bag.

"Come on." Casey grabbed Leanne's hand and pulled her through to the front bedroom. They peered out of the window at the street below.

"That's not his car," Leanne said. She crouched down, and grabbed Casey's sleeve, pulling her down too.

Peering out, they watched two young men exit the car. They looked around the street, and then up at Casey's house.

"Do you know them?" Leanne whispered.

Casey shook her head.

"There's no way it's just a coincidence that they turned up here. They must be looking for you."

"Why?"

"You came back, Casey. You're pretty special."

"Did we shut the front door?"

Leanne thought for a moment. "I honestly can't remember."

"We can go out of the back."

"There's a pile of furniture up against the back door."

"There's an exit from the basement. I think we'll be able to get through. Dad didn't like us going down there, but there's a hole in the hedge at the end of the garden, Liam made it. It leads onto some wasteland."

Leanne offered a tight smile. "Let's give it a go."

The basement was dark, and dusty, and damp. Illuminated with the light on Leanne's phone, they looked at piles of boxes, heaps of blankets, stacks of picture frames. Forgotten toys filled one corner, retired chairs another. Tools and pots and pans dangled from nails driven into the beams above their heads, rocking gently back and forth like Damocles' sword. Leanne watched them warily, involuntarily hunching, bracing for impact.

"The door's back here," Casey whispered.

Leanne followed her between the mountains of stuff collected over a lifetime. Memories, heirlooms, keepsakes. Evidence that lives were lived. Casey seemed coolly unaffected by it, while Leanne found herself lamenting over the histories of people she didn't even know.

"Dad kept the key in one of these old paint pots," Casey said, scrabbling around the shelves. "He kept a lot of other crap too, though." After a while of delving her hand in and out of pots, she exclaimed "Aha," and held a key aloft.

She jiggled it in the lock, leaning hard against the wooden door. It looked like it hadn't been opened in years, and Leanne hoped they wouldn't find it sealed shut, or the hinges rusted through.

Casey grabbed the handle and leaned back, pulling it with all of her weight. With a crack, it shifted, and then clattered against the uneven ground as Casey pulled it open further.

"Come on," she said. "If they're in the house they'll have heard that."

Taking hold of Leanne's hand, Casey set off at a run across the overgrown garden. At the back corner, she plunged into the hedge, the hole still accessible behind a year-or-so's new growth. On the wasteland beyond, she leapt across the rutted ground while Leanne stumbled and tripped along behind her.

The uneven terrain finally gave way to a car park, and Leanne found her feet again. They skidded around the back of a building, and threw themselves to the ground behind some bins.

Breathing hard, Casey began to laugh; the sound of it coughing out between deep gulps of air. Leanne joined in, and the two of them gasped for breaths as they crowed with hysteria.

"Who were those guys?" Casey asked.

Leanne opened her eyes. "I don't know. Who even knows that you're here? Other than me and Mr Hendricks."

"You don't think—"

"No, absolutely not."

"People do crazy things when they're angry."

"No. He was pinning all of his hopes on you. He thought that, if he could find out what happened to you, he could somehow work out when his family were coming home. He'd never risk that chance by telling someone about you, no matter how angry he was." Leanne clamped her hands over her mouth. "My poster," she muttered from behind her fingers.

"What?"

She dropped her hands. "My poster. Oh my God, we made a found poster for you when you first showed up and plastered it all over Chatstone in the hopes of finding your family." She dropped her head into her hands. "They were probably The Arcane."

"The Arcane?"

"The gang that runs Chatstone now. My brother's part of it. And they'd be very interested in you."

"But how did they know where I lived?"

Leanne shrugged. "We didn't know it then. I just put the church address on the posters. Oh my God, Neil."

"Who's Neil?"

"The guy at the church. I put the church address for information about you because I didn't want to risk people coming to my house looking for you. What if they hurt him? What if..." She couldn't bring herself to finish the sentence. "We need to get back to Chatstone."

"If they got to him, there's nothing you can do anyway. We should stay put. In case Mr Hendricks comes back."

Leanne pushed herself to her feet. "I need to see that Neil's alright. I have to. There's nothing in Harroton for us, and it doesn't feel safe here. Especially if that was The Arcane at your house. I put Neil in danger when he's only ever been kind to me. One way or the other, I have to know what happened to him."

23

Leanne zipped up her hoody and pushed her hands deeper into the pockets. October was really taking hold now, and it had brought along a wind which bit at the fingers.

As they walked below grey skies, Chatstone seemed like an impossible distance away. She glanced at Casey, similarly huddled into her jacket, shoulders hunched against the cold and the prospect of a long walk.

"Tell me more about Poisonmarch," Leanne said.

Casey looked up at her. "I don't really know."

"Did they say anything else about it? Or this termination?"

Casey took a deep breath. "They said they've been watching us for centuries, and that we're no longer of any use. Whatever that means."

"Watching us?"

"They said they created us."

Leanne swallowed hard. "Are they, like, Gods of some sort?"

"Not how I'd imagine Gods to be."

"Did you see them?"

Casey shook her head. "Not clearly. Just shadows. Huge eyes. Tentacles, I think. I sensed them more than saw them. But, yeah, they said they made us, and watched us. Looked after us, or, more like, nudged us in this direction, or that direction. Kind of making us do stuff, but not completely controlling us. Does that make sense?"

"Yeah. Like, when you get a feeling in your gut. An instinct. I guess that was them?" Leanne shook her head. "It's so far-fetched," she said quickly. "It's really hard to believe something like that."

Part of her fought to deny it, to dismiss it, but another saw the look in Casey's eyes. A conviction that couldn't be so easily rejected. Her knees weakened beneath her, and she pressed her hands into fists to keep herself from losing all sense of dominion over her body.

"I know, right?" Casey said.

"So much for free will." She cleared her throat to try and shed the waver from her voice. "I mean, I've never been sure of what I believed. I find it hard to accept that the world, you, me, all of our thoughts and feelings, that all of that only exists by chance, by certain atoms colliding, or whatever. I guess I always felt like life had a purpose, which, in turn, I suppose, suggests some kind of higher power. I don't know."

She clamped her mouth shut before more nervous ramblings escaped from it.

"Whatever I thought, I never expected monsters," Casey said.

Leanne choked out a laugh. "Definitely not. Although, I never really believed the depiction of angels; guys with robes and shining wings blowing trumpets, but, yeah, never imagined monsters. I guess humans created what they wanted to be true, what they hoped for. I'd rather have guys in robes than terrifying creatures."

She looked at Casey again, and longed to touch her, to feel her solidity. She needed to know that the world was real around her. She stopped, grabbing hold of a railing. Her head spun, and she leaned heavily against the cold metal.

"Are you alright?" Casey asked.

Leanne nodded. "It's just a lot to take in." She gulped back a lump of tears.

"I guess I've had a lot longer to get used to it."

Leanne glanced up at her. "Were you aware of how long you were there?"

"It kind of just felt like forever."

"Did you think about your family?"

"Nothing else," she said flatly. "But then, real life started to feel more and more distant. More like a dream, I guess. Like it may have never happened at all." She looked down at her feet. "I thought that, maybe, I'd just imagined it all. And now that I'm back here, I'm not even sure which world feels more real to me. Theirs, or ours."

Feeling steadier, Leanne pushed herself upright, just keeping her fingertips on the railing. She still needed that sense of solidity in the world. She wasn't ready to let it go yet.

"I kind of thought," Casey continued, "that when I got home, and saw my mum, that everything would be alright. That all the confusion would disappear, and that seeing my family would make this world real again. But..." She drew in a long breath and let it out slowly. "Maybe I'll never be certain."

"I'm sorry they weren't still here. Did any of them disappear, y'know, before you did?"

Casey shook her head.

"Because, they may have afterwards, I guess there's no way of knowing. Or they just went away somewhere."

"It looks like everyone in Harroton went away somewhere."

"You're right. This place looks like it's completely deserted. It's totally different to Chatstone. We seem to be holding things together, kind of. So, maybe your family upped and left. Have you got any relatives nearby, anyone they might have gone to be with?"

Casey shrugged. "I have a grandmother who lives in Spain, but I've only ever met her the once. And an Uncle in London somewhere, but I've never met him. Maybe all of my family disappeared like me. Maybe everyone in Harroton did."

Leanne slowly lifted her fingers from the railing, testing the strength and tenacity of her legs to stand by themselves.

"It's possible," Leanne said. "But I haven't heard of entire families disappearing before. It was always just some people." She glanced up at the clouds above them. "Like they really knew how to hurt us." She gripped hold of the railing again. "They always left someone behind to suffer." She leant her hip against the metal and breathed hard.

"Like your Mr Hendricks?"

Leanne nodded, gulping in air.

"Do you think he'll come back?" Casey asked.

"I don't know."

"He was pretty angry, all red and shaking. I thought he was going to have a heart attack or something." She laughed.

Leanne shook her head. "I think he was more scared than angry."

"If only we had his phone number."

"No use. The phones don't work anyway." Her face lit. "Or, actually, they are starting to come back." She slipped her phone from her pocket. "I'll call my brother."

"Didn't you say he was in that gang? Can we trust him?"

Leanne lifted her hand from the railing and placed it on Casey's shoulder.

"I promise," she said. "We can trust him."

She flicked to her list of recent calls. A few entries down was her mum. They'd spoken the morning that she'd disappeared. Leanne remembered the conversation; her mum checking that she was on her way to school. She had snapped back at her, saying that she wasn't a child anymore. It had been unusual for her mum to call. Almost like she knew... She shook the thought from her head and clicked on Joel's name. It rang once before disconnecting. She tried again, but the result was the same.

"I'll keep trying," she said.

"What if those guys from the gang drive past and see us?"

Leanne looked around. "It's so quiet, we should hear them coming long before they see us."

"I don't know. Once we hit the main road, it's completely straight. Perhaps we should stay off it."

"I was hoping Mr Hendricks would come back for us. He needs to be able to find us."

"Then why don't we go back to my house?"

"It's not safe. You know that."

"They found it empty. What reason do they have to stick around? And if Mr Hendricks does come back looking for us, that's where he'll go first."

"I don't know. I think it's too dangerous. The whole of Harroton feels unsafe. It gives me the creeps."

"How about we go into one of the other houses, where we have a good view of my house and the road?"

Leanne nodded. "Ok. That sounds sensible. Besides, I didn't really fancy walking all the way back to Chatstone."

24

Leanne had carried a creaky and slightly unstable dining chair upstairs to the front bedroom, and positioned it by the window. She sat, idly watching the road below, while Casey wandered around downstairs.

The car that had pulled up outside Casey's house had disappeared, but that was no guarantee that it wouldn't return, or that no one else would come.

There was also the question of how long they waited in hope of Mr Hendricks' return. He might never come back. He might have crashed his car on the way back to Chatstone, whether deliberately or not. It had so often felt like he was on edge of that, his sanity precarious and delicate, as if just a slight nudge would topple him completely. Maybe this revelation had been all the nudge he needed.

Leanne peered up at the cloud-encased sky. She

tried to imagine the creatures beyond it, but always came back to the chocolate-box idea of heaven; fluffy clouds, golden gates, harps and trumpets. It was too deeply ingrained in her.

Casey clattered into the bedroom with her arms loaded. She dropped what she was carrying onto the floor, and sat herself, cross-legged, next to the pile.

"Entertainment," she said with a wide grin. "I found some grotty romance novels. They're pretty funny in parts. A jigsaw of the London skyline, and another one of Heinz cans and bottles. They look like all the pieces might be there. And I found some old comics. Very old. Probably some of the kind that are worth a fortune. There was a box of action figures too, we could break them out if we get really bored."

Leanne managed a half-hearted smile. "Good job."

Casey sighed. "Yeah, I'm hungry too. But the kitchen was empty. The water's still on though, amazingly."

"What I wouldn't give to just order out for pizza right now," Leanne said, tapping her phone.

"Yeah, right. Or fish and chips."

Leanne waggled a warning finger at Casey. "Don't even start, we'll just drive ourselves crazy."

"Have you tried your brother again?"

"Several times. Still can't get through."

After a moment, Casey said "Pass me that map, I just want to check something."

Leanne fished it from her bag and handed it over. She watched as Casey located the three spires, drawing her fingers into the centre of the triangle. She leaned forward and peered at where her finger was pointing.

"What's there?" asked Leanne.

Casey shrugged. "Just a street."

Leanne turned back to the window. "It was an interesting thought, though."

"Holwell Gardens," Casey said.

"Hold on. Holwell? That means there used to be a well there."

"A well?"

"Yeah, old wells are all over the place. Some of them are obvious, or made into some kind of feature or landmark, while others are underground. You'd never even know they were there except for the name of the street."

"Do you think it's important?"

"It's a pretty big coincidence if it's not. There can't be many in Harroton, it's not that big."

"We should check it out then," Casey said, jiggling up and down excitedly.

"What if Mr Hendricks comes back?"

Casey cocked her head. "Seriously? You saw how angry he was. He's not coming back."

Leanne nodded. Casey had said it with such assurance, so matter-of-factly, and it only echoed what Leanne already felt. She nodded again and stood up. "Ok then. Let's check it out."

Holwell Gardens was a pleasant, if unspectacular, place. A narrow, serpentine road, with terraced houses huddled along one side, their front doors opening right onto the pavement, and a row of allotments opposite. At least, they used to be allotments. They had since drowned under a sea of weeds and brambles, their sheds rising up like islands.

Leanne looked up and down the empty road. She looked at Casey, whose blank, slightly confused face, matched her own.

"There's nothing here," Casey said. "I was kind of expecting..."

"I know. Maybe the open jaws of hell, or something, at least. But, nothing?"

"There's no clue as to exactly where the well is, either. Or was. Hand me the map. Have you got a pen?"

"Sure." Leanne pulled the map from her bag, and dug through for her pencil case. Casey perched on the low wall that edged the allotments, tucking herself between the bramble tendrils.

"I'm going to try Joel again," Leanne said, waving her phone at Casey.

Casey nodded, but her focus was already on the map.

Wandering back up the narrow road, Leanne selected Joel's name from her call list. It rang twice, three times, and then his voice.

"Leanne?"

"Oh thank God! I've been trying to get through to you for ages."

"Are you alright?"

"Umm… something happened. I'm stuck in Harroton."

"Harroton? How did you even get there?"

"Mr Hendricks brought us, but then he left us here. Look, Joel, there's this girl, Casey—"

"Casey? The girl that came back?"

"How do you know about her?"

"The Arcane are going crazy trying to find her. Seriously, Leanne, tell me you're not really with her."

"Yes, I am. Joel, she's told me loads about the things that took her. They're like these monsters that have been watching over us." The words began to tumble out of her, carrying with them a flood of relief. She had needed to get them out, to share the weight of them.

"Woah, Leanne, slow down. Think about this. Don't you think it's odd that she knows so much? Why would these creatures, or whoever or whatever they are, tell all of their plans to a kid they didn't even want to keep hold of?"

"Maybe they sent her back as a messenger."

"Or maybe she's lying to you. Maybe she did bring their thing back, or maybe she's one of them."

"She's just a kid, Joel."

"How can you be so sure?"

"Because I'm with her, and talking to her. You haven't even met her."

"Where are you? I'll get someone to pick you up."

"I'm not telling you."

"Leanne."

"We're figuring this out, Joel. We've found

something, and we're going to check it out."

"Leanne, seriously. Whether she's just an innocent kid or not, there's a lot of people looking for her, and not just The Arcane. You're putting yourself in danger just by being with her."

"Who else is looking for her?"

"Just tell me where you are." His voice was becoming shrill.

"Who else is looking for her, Joel?"

He didn't reply. Leanne took her phone from her ear and checked the screen, thinking she'd been cut off. She put it back to her ear.

"The army," he said quietly.

"The army? What do they know about it?"

"Because she's not the only person that's come back."

25

Leanne wandered back to Casey with her head buzzing. For the second time that day, her legs shook beneath her. She bit down on one side of her tongue, the pain reminding her that this world was real, and she was real, and she needed to keep a grasp on that.

Casey was waiting for her, hopping from foot to foot. "Did you get through to your brother?" she asked.

"Yeah, for a bit, but we could barely hear each other."

"So, he's not coming for us?"

"No. But, I'm not sure we can trust him after all. We're better off on our own."

"Ok. Check this out. I drew lines to the centre of the triangle, so we can pinpoint it exactly. It's just round the corner. Want to look?"

Leanne nodded, pushing her conversation with

Joel to the back of her mind. "Come on then."

They walked down the road together, and as they rounded the corner, they saw a large drain in the middle of the road.

"That must be it," Casey called out. She ran over to it, and crouched down, her fingers scrabbling at the edges of the metal grate. "How do we lift it?" she asked, looking up at Leanne.

"You're not thinking of going down there, are you?"

"Why not?"

"Erm, rats, sewage, drowning, snakes. Possibly alligators." Leanne counted them off on her fingers.

Casey waved a hand at her. "They only have alligators in America."

"Are you sure?" Leanne looked down at the grate again.

"Yes, yes. I think it's all just stories anyway. Help me look for something to lever it up with."

With a frown, Leanne turned and looked around them. Her eyes settled on the tangled mess of allotments. "There's bound to be tools in those sheds," she said.

"Good thinking," said Casey. "See what you can find."

With her arms scratched by brambles, Leanne took hold of the door handle of the first shed she came to, and pulled hard. She leaned back with her weight, willing the bolt or the wooden door itself to break before she did. Her feet skidded on loose gravel, she adjusted her grip, and heaved again.

Something popped, gave way a little, but she honestly couldn't tell if it was the door, or her own shoulder. Straightening, she looked around her. A small, stone wheelbarrow, overflowing with weeds, sat by the corner of the shed. Grabbing it, she swung and slammed it against the door's padlock.

The impact knocked the wheelbarrow from her grip, and it flew to the floor, one of its handles shooting off into the greenery.

There was a large dent in the door, but the padlock still held its sentry.

"Are you kidding me?" Leanne cried out, rubbing her grazed hands on her trousers.

"Are you ok?" called Casey.

"Just having a bit of trouble getting into the sheds," Leanne replied over her shoulder.

"Well, don't worry about it, I've managed to get the grate up anyway."

"Really?"

Leanne pushed her way back through the vegetation, swung her legs over the wall, and dropped back into the street.

The grate was sitting on the road, next to what was now a gaping hole.

Leanne looked up and down the street. "How the hell did you move it?"

Casey shrugged and gave an awkward smile. "It was a lot lighter than I expected it to be."

Leanne looked at it again, the metal several inches thick. She frowned, and switched her gaze to Casey's scrawny arms, her slight frame. She shook her head. "Whatever then."

Kneeling down, she peered into the darkness of the hole.

"What can you see?" Casey asked, peering over her shoulder.

"Nothing. But I can hear the water. It's moving really fast. It's an underground stream."

"That'll be it. That's the well."

"I guess." Leanne placed her hands on the ground as her head started to spin. Her vision darkened, and the rush of water roared through her brain. She felt like she was moving with it, racing along through the dark tunnels, spinning, under the water, breaking free, under the water again. Her mouth gaped uselessly, the air suddenly too thick for her to breathe. And then she was tumbling, tumbling forward through the darkness. Falling. As she landed in the cold water below, her back still tingled from the pressure of the two hands that had pushed her.

26

She stumbled forward, her eyes useless in the darkness, her feet sloshing through the water. Then hands grabbed her, and pulled her upwards. They were strong, and unyielding. They didn't slip or scramble, they pulled her up with complete assurance.

On her knees, she bowed forward and placed her forehead against the ground, steadying the dizziness in her head. She breathed hard, and her body shivered violently.

A hand rubbed her back. She slowly lifted her head, and squinted into the darkness.

A faint glow now surrounded her, curved around her, just tiny flickers of light. They gradually grew in brightness and Leanne got the sense of figures standing around her. They each held two lights, and they grew brighter and brighter, until the tunnels were lit like daylight, the figures masked by the glare.

Leanne blinked and knelt up. A hand reached out to her, and helped her to her feet. She dipped her head; the tunnel only just tall enough for her to stand upright, the damp, dripping curve of it brushing against her hair.

Their song began as a hum, no louder than the rush of the water, or perhaps it began as part of that sound, rising out of it like droplets lifting up in the sunshine. And those droplets saturated the walls, Leanne's skin, her hair. They hung heavy in the air she breathed, sucked onto her lips, and into her lungs.

It was unsettling, in the way that it was meant to be comforting, but it was too out of place to lose its sinister edge. Like the crackle and hiss of a record player in an empty house. Like the feeling you weren't alone when you knew you should be.

Leanne wrapped her arms tightly around herself, and instinctively took a step back. She was aware that the river was not far behind her, she could feel the chill of it on her back, but she couldn't turn around, couldn't remove her gaze from the lights which were now swinging and moving in hypnotic rhythm.

As the lights stilled, and faded, Leanne could finally make out the figures that held them. Except they weren't holding the lights, the lights were inside their hands, under the skin of their palms. And that skin was white, translucent, pearlescent. Each of them shimmered in a different hue; one slightly blue, another lilac, another yellow. There was something less than solid about them; their silhouettes seemed to be slightly fluid, constantly shifting, like they hadn't quite decided what shape they wanted to be.

Leanne took another step back, but it wasn't so much fear, it was more disbelief that moved her. Awe even. She couldn't shake the thought that, if she did believe in angels, this is what she'd imagine them to be like.

She jumped as a hand slipped into hers, and Casey stepped up next to her, a grin spread across her face. "We found them," she said.

"You knew about this?" Leanne's voice came out as little more than a squeak.

Casey shrugged. "Kind of."

"And you didn't warn me?"

"Would you have believed me?"

Leanne kept her eyes focussed on Casey. The sight of her made the world spin a little slower. "I don't know. I've been expected to believe a lot of new things today."

"Anyway, I didn't know exactly what we'd find. I just had a feeling that it was important. That we had to come. Something was pulling me."

Casey squeezed her shoulders up, apparently out of excitement. Leanne felt sick. Over the past two years, her whole life had flipped, and she felt like she was still falling out of it. This must have been how Alice felt tumbling into Wonderland.

"You must have a lot of questions," said the figure next to them.

Leanne took a deep, shaking breath before

looking up at it. Him. Perhaps. She nodded.

"Then let me explain," it said. "Your idea of creation is right, more-or-less, but your naive imagery is incorrect. Of course, it was the natural choice for you, to create some kind of master who looked like yourselves. It's comforting, and far easier to accept than the truth. The truth is often hard to accept. We," he swept his arms around in an arc, gesturing to all of the creatures before them, "are the Ancienteye. In your language, at least. We've had a million names before, and we'll have a million more, if we're lucky. We reside in, what you would translate as, the Levels. Below your world, if you like, although, when everything is spherical, the idea of either up or down is nothing more than a simplification to help you make sense of direction. That's alright. We'll stick with that analogy if it's easier for you. Your world, the Middle Circle, sits between the Levels, and the Heights. The creatures residing there are the Edgefear." He sighed. "They named themselves, as they've named everything that you know."

"They created us," Leanne mumbled.

"And not in their own image," the Ancienteye confirmed. "More in ours, as a matter of fact. I suppose it was some kind of joke. But, they did make you from their own DNA."

Leanne's head flicked up. "We're part of them?"

"Everything in the Middle Circle is. The animals, the plants, the oceans, the mountains, the wind. It's all part of them. Which is why they took so many of you." He sighed again, deeply, drawing the breath out.

"We're dying. Us, the Edgefear. We're facing our own extinction. A disease is spreading through us, we call it the Poisonmarch. The Edgefear took your people in the hope of finding a cure. They won't give up. Not until they've taken every life from the Middle Circle, or until they're extinct themselves."

"So that's it? Our lives mean that much less than their own?"

"Human lives are of very little consequence, if of any consequence at all."

"Well, they're of great consequence to us."

"And do you cry when you squash an insect? Their lives are of great consequence to them. It's nothing more than a matter of perspective. After all, you value the life of a dog differently to that of a pig."

"And we're just spare parts, is that it? Then why even make us conscious? Why give us lives?"

"Just a way to pass the millennia."

"Did it work? Did they find a cure?"

"Their trials have proved fruitless to date."

"Good. I hope you all die. Them, and you." She turned to Casey. "Let's get out of here."

"And go where?" Casey asked.

"Anywhere. We're not going to find any satisfactory answers here."

"What makes you think there are any?" asked the Ancienteye. "Sometimes things just are."

Turning sharply around, turning her back on the Ancienteye, their lights, and their indifference, Leanne stormed off into the tunnels. After a moment, Casey's footsteps rattled behind her.

"Do you even know where you're going?" Casey gasped.

"Why did you bring me here?"

"It's freezing down here, and we're running around getting wet."

"What was the point?"

"I don't know. I just wanted you to see."

Leanne stopped and turned to her. "See what? That all of this is even more hopeless than I could have imagined?" She leant back against the curve of the tunnel and screamed into her hands. "They don't even care about us." The tears came without reserve, hollowing Leanne's chest with desperate gasps for breath. "We really are all alone. There's no one watching over us, no one taking care of us. All we have is ourselves. All we can rely on is ourselves. I'm completely alone."

"You're not completely alone. You still have Joel. Mr Hendricks has no one." Casey leant against the other side of the tunnel, dropping back against the wet bricks heavily. "And neither do I."

Leanne looked at her, and her stomach felt emptier than ever. She stared down at her feet and rubbed at the back of her arched neck. How could she be so thoughtless? So self-absorbed? She lifted her eyes and looked up and down the featureless tunnel.

"What do we do now?"

"Find our way back to the surface, I guess," Casey replied.

"Back to the Middle Circle," Leanne muttered.

Casey slipped her hand into Leanne's. "Don't

worry, we'll find our way out."

They walked without any sense of direction; each tunnel was identical to any that it intersected, leaving them to simply choose their route at random. They walked for several hours, splashing through water, flinching with every drip that hit the backs of their necks, huddling into the inadequate glow that Leanne's phone offered them.

"We're completely lost," Leanne finally whispered.

"We'll find our way."

"What if we're simply going round in circles?"

Casey laid her hand against Leanne's chest, bringing her to a halt. "Pray with me."

"Are you crazy?"

Casey shrugged. "It can't hurt."

"It can't help either. Even if those creatures can actually hear us, we know they don't care. There's no one to help us."

"Then, ignore them. We'll pray to God, just like we used to."

Leanne stamped on through the water, leaving Casey behind her. She could hear her praying, asking for help from a deity they knew didn't exist. Her knees gave way at the reality of it, and her hands scrabbled at the tunnel walls to keep her body upright. The world she'd thought she knew, that had once seemed so solid, so reliable, was nothing more than mist now. That mist was dispersing, and the view beyond was terrifying.

"Come on," she barked over her shoulder. "These

tunnels can't go on forever."

Casey ran to catch her, sending water sloshing up both of their legs. They walked on, coming to another intersection. Leanne stopped. Casey slipped past her and turned left.

"This way," she said, with cheery assurance.

Leanne shrugged and followed. The tunnels were all identical, what difference did it make?

As they rounded a corner, they saw something Leanne had almost stopped believing in. Daylight. The tunnel ahead of them widened, and led straight out into the world. The girls took deep gulps of the fresh air as they emerged into the chill of dusk.

The sky above them was deep purple, with the first stars peppered across it. At the horizon, a strip of low clouds glowed pink, like candyfloss.

The world was just how they'd left it. It didn't know what they knew, and in its ignorance, it continued to be as beautiful as it ever had been. As beautiful as it had been when Leanne believed it might have been lovingly pieced together by hands she recognised, hands like hers. Hands that cared about such things. But it wasn't. It had been thrown together by creatures who valued nothing but their own existence. The beauty wasn't intentional, it wasn't in place to inspire mankind, or fill them with wonder, or awe. To bring them to their knees to thank God for his wondrous bounty. It was a happy accident, a by-product of the rising and setting sun.

Casey slipped her hand into Leanne's and gazed up at the sky.

Perhaps it wasn't so haphazard after all. Perhaps the world created it out of defiance. Refusing to be nothing more than the sum of its parts. Perhaps the world found its own purpose in creating its own beauty.

Suddenly, Casey let out a loud howl, her head tipped back, her mouth open towards the sky, as if she were trying to swallow it whole. Leanne smiled, and dropped her own head back. She screwed her eyes closed as she joined in, and tears flowed from them, pooling into her ears. She howled for her parents, for Joel, for herself. She howled for Mr Hendricks, for his girls, his wife. She howled for Casey and her whole family. For her lost friend, Sophie, and her parents, and the looks on their faces. Neil, his church, and all of the missing posters. For the life she'd had; the places she used to go to, the cinema, the shopping centre, the fast food restaurants. For everything she had once taken for granted. Not because she didn't care, or didn't appreciate it, but because she thought it was forever. Because she couldn't have imagined a life without it. She dropped to her knees, screaming as she pounded her fists against the ground. She screamed for the parents who had always seemed like a constant, an irremovable certainty. Immortal. They weren't supposed to leave her, they weren't allowed to. She wasn't meant to be left behind. Not by them.

Dropping forward, she placed her forehead against the ground, laying her palms by her ears. She breathed hard, her lungs struggling for the space they needed. Casey rubbed her bowed back.

"It worked. We found our way out. Everything's going to be fine now. You see?"

Leanne sat up and looked at Casey. "No, I don't see," she said. "I don't understand any of this. When I woke up this morning, in my own bed, with a vague, if unrecognised, belief in God, I thought I knew what the world was about. And I still had hope that the universe was looking out for us. That, somehow, it would set things right. That I'd hear a key turn in the front door, and my parents would walk in and everything would be normal again. Life would be normal again."

"And now?"

"Now I know that all we have is monsters, who don't give a shit. That all we are is spare parts and entertainment. That life is completely pointless. That it was nothing more than a happy accident that we found our way here." She looked down at the ground. "And I know that my parents are never coming home." She sighed. "And that we have absolutely no idea where we are."

"I guess we should find somewhere to spend the night." Casey looked around the empty field. There were no buildings in sight, no roads, no hint of mankind beyond the tunnels they'd just crawled out of.

Deep black against the sunset, a thick line of trees huddled together. Casey pointed.

"There. At least there'll be some shelter if it rains."

Leanne pushed herself to her feet. "It's as good a plan as any, I guess."

They trudged across the rutted ground, stumbling in the darkness over tussocks and slipping into trenches.

"It'll be a bloody miracle if neither of us break an ankle. Or two," Leanne muttered.

She looked up at the shadowy trees, and swallowed back the fear that rose from her stomach like bile. She wanted buildings, street lights, signs of human life. The tight cluster of black trees was not her idea of sanctuary for the night.

Her foot hit another tussock, and propelled her forward, her arms wheeling.

"Hey! Watch out!" the tussock said. And then it scrambled to its feet, and took on the shape of a man.

Leanne had read so many books where the hero was frozen with fear, or there was an agonizing wait for their body to catch up with their brain, but that wasn't how it happened. Leanne's body reacted before she even realised, taking off towards the trees faster than she even knew she could run. She heard feet pounding behind her, but she didn't know if it was Casey or the tussock man following her. She didn't turn to look. She kept her eyes focussed on the dark line of trees, their shadows finally becoming a tempting prospect.

She didn't make it to the trees. Her feet lifted from the ground as the man grabbed her, his arm slipping under her arms, and wrapping tightly around her chest.

27

Leanne kicked and struggled, her heel finally making contact with shin. The man winced, bending forward suddenly, crushing Leanne in his grip. She kicked again, but her foot found only space this time.

"Stop," the man grunted into her ear. "I don't want to hurt you, but I'm armed, and I will shoot you if I have to."

Leanne went limp, her exhaustion pushing past her panic.

"Please, don't make me hurt you." He shifted his grip on her. "I'm going to put you down now, with your friend. I will shoot you if you run. Understand?"

Leanne nodded. Her feet made contact with the ground again, and the man released her. Casey was sitting on the floor, and Leanne settled next to her, looking up at the large gun pointing at them. Leanne realised that she'd never seen a gun before, not in real life. Even as the man lowered it to his side, its ominous eye staring only at the ground, she could still feel the impact of its gaze.

"Who are you?" he asked them.

Leanne turned to Casey and shook her head, a tiny, tight movement.

"What are you doing out here at night?" The man sighed. "I know, I know, you're being cautious. You don't know who I am. That's sensible. That will help you a lot."

Leanne looked him up and down. He didn't look like he was many years older than Joel. The hair growth that shaded his chin appeared soft, fluffy, like that on the faces of Joel's friends. Not like the harsh bristle her father had rubbed against her cheek; a joke that never seemed to lose its hilarity for him. The lad's hair looked like it had been cropped close to his head once, but it had grown too long, into no particular kind of style. He wore a dark green t-shirt with matching combat trousers, covered in pockets. They all looked to be filled with something bulky.

"You should be careful," he continued, "because it's dangerous out here. Especially after dark."

"How can it be?" Leanne asked, feeling suddenly brave in the realisation of his juvenile status. "There's no one out here."

"I'm out here."

"But, you said you wouldn't hurt us," Casey pointed out.

"No, I said that I didn't want to hurt you. Not that I wouldn't. If you're quiet, and well-behaved, then you have nothing to fear. Not from me, anyway. But out there," he cocked his head towards the trees, "you have everything to fear."

Leanne turned away so that he couldn't see her smirking. This new world was filled with boys who thought they were heroes, bolstering their image with snippets of speech lifted from bad movies and trashy TV shows. Is this all the future had to offer?

"What's in the trees?" Casey asked, an edge of sarcasm evident in her tone.

"You've not been out much after dark, have you?"

"No," Leanne replied. "We're still observing our curfews."

"Well, you're lucky. Look up."

Leanne and Casey both dropped their heads back and gazed up at the dark sky above. Among the stars, a huge streak of light stretched across the sky. It was wide, and bright, its edges jagged as if the sky had been torn open.

"What the hell is that?" Leanne asked. She instinctively pushed herself backwards, as if she could somehow distance herself from it.

"We don't know. We call it 'the rip'. It appeared about a week ago. It's barely even visible during the day, nothing more than a grey smudge. But at night..." He gestured upwards with his free hand.

Casey looked at Leanne with wide eyes, her hand resting gently on Leanne's arm. "The Poisonmarch is coming."

28

In any other circumstances, the sausages and beans that had been squeezed out of a sealed bag would have been one of the least appetising things Leanne had ever seen. But, with her stomach empty, the army-issued rations, despite their bland flavour and unappetising spongy texture, seemed like the best thing she'd ever tasted. Casey equally gobbled down the offerings, accepting the additional high-energy biscuits without hesitation.

Leanne glanced up at their host, who watched them with amusement. He'd introduced himself as Kenton, a soldier. Leanne had been right; he was barely two years older than Joel, and he'd been a soldier for less time than Leanne had been without her parents.

"You two really were hungry," he said. "Tea? Or coffee? I think I've got some hot chocolate here

141

somewhere, if you prefer." He pulled a large rucksack towards him and began digging out more packets of food.

Casey looked up from her meal, her eyes lighting. "Hot chocolate?"

Kenton grinned broadly, a full, clumsy smile that gave him the look of a little boy. It was a dangerous smile; the kind that evoked trust, and encouraged an underestimation of him. He wasn't a little boy, Leanne reminded herself, he was a trained soldier with a big gun.

Kenton unfolded his legs and stepped down from the back of the Land Rover they were all huddled in. He had a small gas stove set up outside, the long grass cleared away in a circle around it.

"So, where are you girls from? I'm from Lancaster, originally. I suppose, these days, I'm not really from anywhere. We've been on the road for so long now, I barely ever know where I am. Where do you girls call 'home'?"

Casey opened her mouth to respond, but Leanne put a warning hand on her leg. Kenton was good; give them food, give them shelter, break down their barriers.

Instead, Leanne replied with her own question. "Did you lose anyone, Kenton? Did any of your family disappear?"

"My big brother, he was one of the first ones to go. I looked up to him so much. He played rugby, was well on his way to doing it professionally." He laughed. "He was a complete asshole though. It couldn't have happened to a nicer person. But, that was what prompted me to join the army, I guess. I saw what it did to my mum, to lose him. Even after millions of people had disappeared, once we knew this was a 'thing', she still kept looking for him, truly believed that he wasn't a part of this. That he was just sleeping on a mate's sofa, or run off with some girl. She withered away under the stress of it all, and I wanted to do something. Maybe save other families from that pain." He shrugged. "I don't know, though. The army's just bumbling around not knowing their arses from their elbows at the moment."

"What about the rest of the world?"

Kenton shrugged again. "Dunno. Last time we had comms, it was going to shit everywhere. Just like here."

"What about the government? Where are they?"

Kenton smiled. "I shouldn't be telling you any of this, you know."

Leanne glanced at Casey. "Two girls? What exactly are we going to do? Start a revolution? I'm just wondering why no one's come to help us."

Kenton nodded. "Fair enough." He poured out the boiling water, and added powdered whitener in place of milk. "They're burning hot, I'll leave them out to cool for a moment." He straightened up, arching his back to stretch it out. "There are some MPs still holding it together, but not many. As far as I know, they're holed up in some bunker somewhere with a 24-7 armed guard. I suppose they're giving some kind of instruction but, really," he smiled grimly, "it's every man for himself out here."

"That's why no one's challenged the gangs."

"A lot of them are doing a damn good job, actually. Keeping things going, keeping things in check. As you can imagine, there are places that it's absolute anarchy." He shuddered. "Some of the things I've heard. Some of the things I've seen." He glanced quickly up at the sky. "People need instructions, they need rules and order."

"So, where have you guys been? Why aren't you sorting everything out?"

"We've all got our own shit to deal with. Just like everyone else."

"And what about your responsibilities?"

"For a lot of people, those responsibilities became null the moment the pay checks stopped coming."

"You're not getting paid?"

"There are no banks anymore. Money has become pretty much worthless. Anyone who's still officially in the army are doing it for their own reasons. Some, because they really believe they're making some kind of difference." He snorted. "Some of them, like me, are still here because they have shit-all idea what the hell else to do. And some... well, they're just bloody pissed off guys enjoying having access to the country's arsenal of weapons. Not the best combination. And we're all hurting, just like you. And we're all scared."

"Don't you just want to go home?" Casey asked. "What about your mum?"

He looked down at the floor and rubbed the back of his neck. "I don't even know what's happened to them; my mum and my little sister. I've not heard from them since we turned all the phone masts off."

"They were turned off deliberately?"

"Orders from above. I guess it was to stop mass panic from spreading, or to stop the gangs coordinating. We've all become so reliant on our phones that, take them down, and comms come to a complete stop. You stop people from getting organised."

"And you stop families being able to find each other," Leanne said.

"I guess it's all for the greater good, or something. We've been turning some of the masts back on, intermittently, just testing the waters. But with what's happening, with the people who've returned, everyone's even more tense than they were before."

Leanne glanced at Casey. The girl's face was tight, her eyes fixed ahead. Her mind was probably racing, just like Leanne's was.

"What's happening to them? The ones that have come back?" Casey asked. Her voice was tiny, but the question was huge.

"They've got labs, scientists. I dunno exactly, but we deliver the ones we can capture, and they do whatever scientists do. Looking for a cure, I guess. Or making sure it can't spread."

"How many of these people have you seen?" Casey leaned forward, her voice heavy with accusation.

"A couple. Believe me, that's enough. It's no surprise that everyone's calling them 'zoms'. It's just like what you see in the movies; rabid, crazy. All claws and teeth."

"And you've personally come face to face with a couple?"

Kenton nodded, a shadow passing over his face.

Casey sat back again, but she was far from satisfied. "And have they found a cure?"

"I would guess not, because now the orders have changed."

"Changed how?"

"The orders aren't to try and capture the zoms anymore, we're under orders to shoot on sight. And shoot to kill."

"And how many of them have you seen come out of those woods?"

"None... yet."

"So, how do you know there are any in there?"

"I don't, I guess. But what does that matter? I have my orders, and I'll stay here until those orders change."

Casey snorted and folded her arms. "Sounds like you're being made a fool of."

"Perhaps, but they're my orders."

"Do you always follow orders?"

"That's what I'm paid to do."

"But you're not being paid anymore."

Kenton gave his boyish smile again, and nodded his head. "You're right there, but the army have worked out their own compensation structure. I'll be looked after for staying loyal."

"Is it worth it? What they've promised you, is it worth killing all those people? People who are loved and missed? People whose families are still hoping they'll come home? People like your brother?"

"I've seen what the zoms are like, what they can do, and, as far as I'm concerned, they're not people anymore. Not like you and me."

"They're more like me than you'd think," muttered Casey.

Leanne shot out her hand and gripped Casey's leg, willing her to stay silent. She looked up at Kenton. "And what if your brother came out of those trees? Would you shoot him too?"

"He's not my brother anymore."

"It's that simple, huh?"

"It's that simple."

Leanne turned away, suddenly repulsed by the sight of that smile. "We'll see."

Kenton clapped his hands together. "Anyway, nice as this is, I have patrols to do. You girls get some sleep, and I'll have breakfast cooking when you wake up, ok?"

Casey and Leanne nodded.

Kenton clambered out of the Land Rover and grabbed his gun, leaning it against his shoulder.

"Seriously, get some sleep. You're two of the safest people in the world right now. Not everyone gets their own personal guard."

He winked, and slammed the back door shut.

29

Leanne groaned and tried to push away the hands that pulled at her. She frowned, still mostly asleep, and tried to roll over, but her arms refused to come with her.

As panic flooded through her body, her eyes snapped open. The world around her was super sharp, every sound amplified, the colours deep and rich. And the sensation of something tightly binding her wrists filled her mind, pushing everything else out.

Arching her back, she screamed.

A hand clamped onto her chin, snapping her head around. She looked up at Kenton, his finger over his lips. He gestured towards the outside of the Land Rover.

Leanne wheeled her eyes around, looking for Casey. She was sitting against the other side of the vehicle, her face a mask of terror.

"Are you going to stay quiet?" Kenton whispered.

Leanne nodded, and he released her, disappearing back into the darkness.

She struggled and squirmed, until she managed to get herself upright, sitting opposite Casey. She opened her mouth to speak, but Casey sharply shook her head, flicking her eyes towards the open back door. There were voices outside. Someone else was here.

Kenton returned and climbed in with them. "We're going for a little drive," he said.

"No," Leanne replied. "No, we're not."

Kenton rolled his eyes and patted his gun. "Yes, we are." He pulled the back door shut.

The cab door opened, and someone climbed in, the vehicle rocking slightly.

"Who's that?" asked Leanne.

"If I'm patrolling all night," Kenton replied, "who do you suppose patrols during the day? I have to sleep, I can't do it all myself." That sickening smile again. "That is Dex."

He turned around and grinned at them. "I'll be your driver today folks." His face was cut across by deep shadow, but he was no older than Kenton. Two boys playing soldiers.

"Better prepare yourselves," Kenton said. "Dex is a shit driver."

"Hold on tight." Dex waggled his hands at them and laughed. "Oops, guess you can't. Good luck then."

The Land Rover lurched forward, and both

Leanne and Casey toppled to their sides.

Kenton laughed.

"We trusted you," Leanne spat at him, struggling to get herself upright again.

He looked away from her, shifting his position.

"Where are you taking us?" she asked.

"Turning you in. Following orders."

"There's quite a bounty on your heads," Dex called from the front seat. "Well, Casey's head at least." He held up a crumpled copy of Leanne's found poster. The ones she'd plastered all over Chatstone. That she'd pinned up in the church.

Leanne stared at her knees, her cheeks tingling. Her throat felt thick, and she ran through every self-loathing phrase she could think of. Why hadn't she considered the consequences? She couldn't be trusted with such decisions. Casey wasn't safe with her. No one was. Her heart began to race as she dug her nails into her clenched palms. Heat flushed through her body, and she snapped her head towards Kenton.

"And you really think they'll pay you? They'll screw you over, just like you did to us. Because that's what kind of shithole world we live in now."

Kenton looked down at her, then raised his eyes back to the windscreen.

"Kenton. She's just a kid."

"No, she's a zom."

"Look at her. You know she's not. She came out of it. What if the others can too? What if they can all be saved?"

Kenton's eyes quivered, but he didn't look at Casey, or back at Leanne. "They can't," he replied. "They can't be saved. Better prepare yourselves, we'll be going fast through the trees. Last thing we want is a zom ambush."

The Land Rover bounced over the ground, furrowed by roots. Leanne tucked her chin to her chest, and tried to keep her legs curled in against her, but the motion tossed her about, bashing her knees and elbows against the side of the truck. Her head struck something hard, and the pain sung in her skull like a ringing bell. She blinked, her vision turning dark at the edges.

"What the—" Dex cried out, and the Land Rover skidded to a stop, throwing all of them forward.

Kenton untangled himself from the girls and crawled forward, leaning to see out of the front. "What the hell is that?"

Leanne rolled over and manoeuvred up onto her knees, craning her neck. In the darkness ahead of them, a curve of lights lit the trees in a soft candle-like glow. The lights were bunched together in pairs, like eyes, watching them, waiting.

Leanne looked at Casey, who was equally straining to see.

Casey turned to her with a smile. "You see," she said. "They do care."

Dex picked up his gun from the passenger seat and swung the door open. He dropped out of the cab and lifted his weapon towards the lights.

"He probably shouldn't do that," Casey said, her

voice light with a tone of amusement.

"Turn those lights out!" yelled Dex. "Who are you?"

The lights grew brighter, and Leanne squinted against their glare.

"Turn those lights out!" Dex screamed. "I will shoot, and I've got a bloody big gun. I'll kill you all."

Leanne closed her eyes to slits as the lights continued to strengthen. Dex lifted his arm over his own eyes.

"I'll kill you!" he yelled. "I'll kill you all!"

When Dex's head exploded, it went with nothing more than a pop. The sound was rather like that of popping a single blister of bubble wrap. But that wasn't the sound that would play over and over in Leanne's memory. It was the spatter of blood across the windscreen, and the clunk of bone hitting the bonnet.

Slowly, shakily, Kenton raised his finger and pointed to where Dex used to be. "What the hell is out there?" he whispered.

"They're here to protect me," Casey said. "So, I suggest you let us go before you end up like your friend."

Kenton nodded quickly. "Sure, sure." Slipping a knife from his belt, he hurriedly cut them both free. "I'm sorry, I'm so sorry, I didn't want to, but Dex— Tell your friends I'm sorry. I'm so sorry."

Leanne rubbed at her wrists, circling her free hands around.

"What are they?" Kenton asked. "What can do

that?"

"The Ancienteye," said Casey.

The back door of the Land Rover flew open, and Kenton fell backwards, scrambling to the other end of the truck.

The Ancienteye surrounded the vehicle, and as they lowered their arms to their sides, the lights faded and went out. One of them stepped forward and stared hard at Kenton, who was now cowering up against the cab. The Ancienteye's gaze ran over him, head to toe, inspecting every part of him.

It turned to the others, the lights in its palms flickering on and off. Others responded with their own lights flashing.

The Ancienteye turned back to Kenton. "You'll come with us, down to the Levels."

"No, no, please," Kenton whimpered. "I'll let them go, you can take them both. I won't even tell anyone that I saw them."

"We didn't come here for them, we came for you?"

"What? Why?"

"Your other... Your like..." The Ancienteye struggled for the right word. "Brother? Yes, brother. The Edgefear found something useful in him. It's likely that it's in you too. And we found you first, so you belong to us. The key to our salvation. Our cure."

30

It had become so dark that Leanne could no longer see Casey sitting opposite her. It was silent too, no wind, no animals, nothing. It was as if the world had ceased to exist outside of the Land Rover.

"I've never felt so alone," whispered Casey. "Even when we went to my house, and we found it abandoned, my whole family gone, even that wasn't as bad as this."

"I know what you mean. It's like being abandoned by God." Leanne wrapped her arms tightly around her aching stomach.

"What do we do now?"

"I have no idea."

They sat in silence for a moment, Leanne trying to find any motivation, any reason to do anything at all. She wasn't sure she had any fight left in her. Maybe they should simply sit, and wait for the end.

Whatever the end might be.

"Do you know how to drive?" Casey asked at last.

"No."

"Do you really think the woods is full of people who've returned? Full of zoms?"

"I don't know. You don't have to call them that, you know. It doesn't seem right." Leanne sighed deeply. "I guess we just lock all the doors and wait until morning. Things might look different in the daylight."

"My mum always said a good sleep solved most problems."

"I think it might take more than that this time."

Casey huffed. "Do you think they will find the cure? That it is in Kenton?"

"I hope not. I hope they all die."

"But then we really will be alone."

"We're better off by ourselves anyway."

Leanne woke to sunshine. It shot through the canopy of trees like darts, lighting the blood on the windscreen, and filling the truck with a rosy glow. She lay her head back down and closed her eyes. And she listened. The world was as silent as it had been last night. No birds singing. No wind, or distant sounds of traffic or church bells. Nothing. Like the world had been emptied out.

She sat up and looked around. The back of the truck was filled with bags and boots, blankets and helmets, guns and knives. These boys had really been living out their commando fantasies.

While Casey slept on, Leanne carefully catalogued the items that would be of use to them. Food packets, packets of water, blankets. She found a map and compass, a GPS tracker. Torches, a small, folding shovel. The boots were far too big for them both, but she took some spare socks and t-shirts. She looked at the thick coats hung up, but they were so heavy. She mentally put them onto the 'maybe' list. The small camping stove was a must. Matches, and a couple of lighters. A small first aid kit, two lightweight ponchos, a whistle.

She looked around at the number of items that she didn't even recognise. She was bound to be leaving something essential behind, through ignorance, but they couldn't carry everything. There was an array of guns, boxes of ammunition, an odd-looking weapon that she assumed was a flare gun.

"What are you doing?" Casey grumbled. She slowly sat up, rubbing her eyes. She looked around as if she'd forgotten where she was. "What are you doing?" she asked again.

"Packing. Just taking useful stuff."

She yawned and arched her body into a stretch that extended through to her fingertips. "What about the guns?" she asked.

Leanne looked around at them again. "Do you know how to use one?"

Casey shook her head.

"Me neither. To be honest, they're just more weight to carry, and we're more likely to accidentally kill ourselves with them than anyone else. We'll just take some knives. At least we don't need instructions for them." Leanne smiled and attempted a laugh. It came out thick and heavy. They had no idea what they were doing, no experience in any kind of survival situation. The worst thing Leanne had ever survived was power cuts and the internet going down. They weren't ready to be the heroes of a post-apocalyptic scenario.

"Did you hear anything during the night?" Casey asked. "Out there?"

Leanne shook her head. "Not a thing. I actually slept right through."

"The silence woke me." Casey smiled awkwardly. "How weird is that? I guess we get used to all the sounds around us, we don't even notice them anymore, but we notice when they're not there." She folded her legs up underneath her. "I'm not sure there are actually any zoms out there."

"Maybe the army sent Kenton and Dex out here to get rid of them."

"That's far more believable than a pack of wild zoms."

They laughed, but it did nothing to lighten the atmosphere.

"What's the plan?" asked Casey.

Leanne shrugged. "I guess we just start walking. If we walk in one direction, we'll eventually hit a road. And all roads lead somewhere."

"And then?"

Leanne chewed her lip. "I guess that's it for now. We'll find a road, figure out where we are, and then we'll decide."

They packed two rucksacks with the supplies Leanne had decided they would take, and hefted them onto their shoulders. Leanne looked longingly at the two heavy coats, but knew that they couldn't carry them.

"Let's go," she said.

They climbed from the back of the Land Rover, and Leanne shut the doors. They stood there for a moment. Just looking. Saying goodbye. Leanne lifted her head towards the woods. The shadows were deep, the floor dappled with abstract flecks of sunshine, like a jigsaw yet to be pieced together. They were alone, and there was no one on their side. Not any more. She glanced at Casey. Just a skinny little girl, her messy hair tied back from her grubby, tear-stained face. And now a fugitive. This isn't what her life was meant to be. This isn't what childhood was meant to be.

"I guess we better get going," Leanne said. "Get some distance between us and this place before it gets dark. They're going to come looking for Dex and Kenton sooner or later."

They wandered around to the front of the vehicle, looking anywhere but at Dex's body.

The woods were cool, and silent. Not a single bird, or rabbit, or mouse. Nothing moved, nothing called out to warn of their presence. Nothing breathed. Even the trees seemed too solid to be living.

When they broke free of the woodland and

stepped into wide, flat fields, Leanne filled her lungs with the open air, breathing in relief, soaking in sunshine.

Casey lifted her face to the sky, closing her eyes against the brightness of it. "We're alive," she whispered. "Despite everything, we're still alive."

Leanne took hold of Casey's hand and squeezed it. "Let's keep it that way."

She looked up at the grey streak across the sky. The Poisonmarch. Kenton had been right; it was barely visible during the day, like a wisp of cloud. A mask of innocence. People had no idea what was coming, or even that anything was coming at all. Their lives had been torn to shreds already, maybe ignorance really was bliss.

She looked across the fields that stretched before them. They could disappear easily enough. Two girls, and the entire country to get lost in. But they'd always be running, always be looking over their shoulders. They couldn't trust anyone. She looked back up at the tear. They were living on borrowed time anyway. Something was going to come through that rip, and when it did, there would be no hiding from it.

31

It was unseasonably warm for October, and with the weight of the rucksacks on their backs, they soon discarded the extra layer of their jumpers, tying them around their waists. But the winter was coming, and it wouldn't stay this warm forever.

Leanne glanced back at shrinking line of the trees, thinking about the thick coats they'd left behind. Perhaps they would have been a better idea than the blankets. Was it too late to go back?

"Do you hear that?" Casey's hand landed on her arm.

They stopped moving, and Leanne listened. Dogs. She turned around, trying to pinpoint the direction of the sound.

"Where are they?" she asked.

"I don't know," said Casey. "But they're a long way off yet. There must be a farm around here somewhere."

"Maybe their owners disappeared. Maybe they're really hungry." She turned and lunged at Casey, as if to bite her. Casey leapt out of her reach, squealing.

"Could they have really survived this long?"

Leanne shrugged. "Depends. If there were chickens, or other small animals, rats maybe. It's certainly possible."

"I guess a lot of animals must have died when their owners disappeared."

"I guess so. But, also, a lot of animals will have survived because of all this."

"Maybe it all balances out then."

"Maybe." Leanne raised her head as the barking started again. "We'll keep listening, steer away from the farm."

Casey snorted out a laugh. "We're looking for a road, for signs of life and people, yet we're also terrified of it all."

Leanne laughed. "Yeah, I guess we're totally screwed. But I do not relish coming across a pack of hungry dogs."

"Maybe it's wolves."

"There aren't any wolves in the UK. I don't think so, anyway. Not wild."

"They might have got out. I mean, there's got to be some zoo keepers who disappeared, right?"

"Do wolves bark? I thought they only howled."

"I don't know."

Leanne tried to dismiss the idea, it just wasn't that logical, but a doubt still clung to her. She seemed to be covered in stubborn doubts that refused to let go, weighing her down, slowing her step.

She looked at Casey. Why did she feel so responsible for this girl? She could have simply walked away, let the army take her, gone back home, thought no more about it. Why did she feel so duty-bound to protect her?

"Hey look!" cried Casey, pointing wildly.

Leanne looked. Ahead of them was a field filled with dandelions, their downy, white heads nodding like old, bearded men taking their afternoon naps.

Casey grinned broadly and slipped her rucksack from her shoulders. Leanne lowered hers to the ground.

"Ready?"

It felt good to run, without purpose, without fear of being caught. Just running free, dancing, skipping. The seeds lifted from the flowers like blossom, filling the air with confetti, spinning around them, running alongside, until the breeze carried them up and out of reach.

Breathless, they dropped to the ground, their hair and clothes covered with snagged seeds.

Casey hollered and whooped, her head arched backwards against the floor.

Leanne breathed hard, her hand resting on her chest, rising and falling with it. She looked at Casey, the grin on her face, her eyes wide and bright. Carefree. That was why she needed to do this, to take care of her: because if Casey lost her childhood, it would be the end of Leanne's too. The end of all innocence in the world. And if Leanne became an adult, became capable and independent, it meant that, even if her parents did come back, she wouldn't need them. She needed to need them. It was the only reason her hope endured. And when people lost hope, death felt too much like a friend.

She rolled onto her side. This moment was one to treasure, and she needed to believe that there would be more moments like this. She needed to keep Casey safe so that there could be. That was the only way to survive in this world; finding something to cling to, a reason to keep fighting, and it had to be compelling enough that you'd never let it go. Casey was her reason, and she would cling to her with every bit of strength she had left.

She sat up, and brushed dandelion seeds from her hair, picked one from her lip.

"That was fun," Casey said.

"It was."

Casey sat up and looked around. "I guess we'd better start walking again."

Leanne nodded and pushed herself to her feet. The air around them was still freckled with the fleece of dandelions. It was too easy to forget that the world still had gifts to offer them.

The dogs barked again, louder than before. They were walking towards them.

Leanne traipsed back up the slope and picked up the two rucksacks. She handed the lighter one to Casey.

"Let's make this as fun as we can," she said.

"Right? We've got to remember to make it fun."

Casey smiled and nodded once, quickly.

"We need to keep an eye out," Leanne continued. "We don't want to get too close to the farm, so we need to make sure we see it before anyone who might be there sees us. It has to be connected to some kind of road somewhere. We'll find our way from there."

"Sounds like a plan." Casey shrugged the rucksack up onto her shoulders, and tucked her thumbs behind the straps. "I'm ready," she announced.

They hadn't gone far when they found themselves stood at the edge of a ridge, the land sloping down and away from them, sweeping into a wide valley. The farmhouse sat at the centre of it.

Leanne crouched down into the long grass, and Casey mirrored her. The farmhouse seemed still enough, but the dogs were barking wildly.

"Do you think they can already smell us?" Leanne asked.

"I dunno. Maybe, I guess."

There were a number of vehicles parked in the farmyard; a tractor, a car, something Leanne didn't even recognise. But there were several vehicles that she recognised all too well.

"Shit." She turned away, as if simply looking elsewhere could make it all disappear. "See the Land Rovers?" she asked Casey. "The army are there. They've probably set it up as some kind of base camp."

"Out here?"

Leanne looked at Casey for a moment. "They're looking for you. They'll be wherever you are."

Casey nodded, her eyes narrowing. "There's the road," she said quietly.

Leanne looked down into the valley to where another Land Rover rattled and bounced along the farm track. "We'll head that way, away from the farm, try to meet the track at the other end, where it joins the road."

"We're always going to be running, aren't we? Always going to be hiding." She rubbed at her nose. "Always scared."

"It makes me realise how safe I felt in Chatstone. I used to walk around there as if nothing had changed. It wasn't like this. People were just the same as they'd always been. As much as I hate to say it, The Arcane were actually doing a good job. Maybe Joel was right."

"Do you think the army will try to take over?"

"Get rid of the gangs? I dunno. Maybe it would depend on how well each gang are looking after things. There's got to be places that aren't working as well as Chatstone. It wasn't just The Arcane in the beginning. There were a few different gangs, fighting for control. That was pretty scary. There were a lot of fights, guns even. God knows where they got them from. I guess people get pretty resourceful when things like this happen." She huffed. "Not that anything like this has happened before, but other disasters, I mean." She picked at a piece of grass, stripping the seeds from it. "Except me. I wasn't resourceful at all. I just kind of carried on, tried to pretend nothing had changed. I just, I guess I stuck my head in the sand. Oh God, Joel took on everything. All the worry, all the danger, and I just played make-believe. He took on all of it, while I did nothing." She dropped her head into her hands. "I've been so selfish."

Casey rubbed her shoulder. "Don't do this to yourself. No one knew what to do, and you just did what you could. You're still just a child, remember."

"So's Joel."

Casey took her hand away. "You can't blame yourself. No one can." She sighed. "No one knew what to do."

Leanne nodded and looked back at the farm. "I guess we'd better get moving. Put as much distance between us and this place as we can."

They stood up and set off across the field, the long grass brushing their fingertips.

"We're so exposed here," Leanne said. She looked back at the farm again. "It only takes someone to be looking in the right direction, and they'll spot us. Bend down. And hurry."

Half-crouching, half-running, they made their way through the grass, disturbing butterflies that should have already gone wherever butterflies went during the winter. It was too warm for October, even nature didn't know what was going on.

"Leanne!"

Leanne froze. Casey continued for a few more

steps before turning back. "What is it?" she whispered.

"Someone called my name," Leanne whispered back. She felt dizzy. "Did you hear it?"

Casey shook her head. "It was probably just the wind."

"Leanne!"

Casey's eyes widened. "I heard that."

Leanne straightened up and turned around. She lifted a trembling hand to her mouth, and, with a grunt, all of the air left her body. She stumbled forward, her arms reaching out.

"Who is it?" Casey's voice seemed distant, insubstantial.

The world was fading around them, and all Leanne could see, the only real thing that still existed, was the dark figure of Joel, waving his arms against the bleached sky behind him.

"Joel!" she wailed, falling into his arms. Her feet scrabbled to find some traction, but her knees refused to hold her. They sank to the ground together, submerged into the swell of grass.

Leanne scrabbled at Joel, as if she were trying to climb into him. He took hold of her hands, and pressed them between his.

"Is it really you?" she gasped.

"It's really me." His voice was tight, barely more than a squeak.

She pulled her hands free from his and clasped them to his face. "It really is. God, I've missed you. Joel, I love you so much."

He smiled awkwardly, his cheeks warming under her hands. She dropped them into her lap and shuffled back from him.

"I'm glad you're still alive," she muttered.

"I'm glad you're alive, too." He clambered back to his feet and glanced behind him.

Leanne stood up and grinned at him, feeling foolish. "How did you find us?" she asked.

He swallowed and pushed his hands into his pockets.

Leanne took a step back, and felt Casey's hand slip into hers. She squeezed it. "How did you find us?" Leanne asked again.

His eyes flicked to one side before focussing on the long grass between them. "I'm sorry," he said.

"What have you done?"

"It was the right thing."

"What have you done, Joel?"

He glanced over his shoulder again, stepping to one side as he did so.

The dogs came first, wet noses snuffling, white teeth bared, straining at their leads, pawing at the ground. Their mouths dripped with saliva, their eyes rolled in their skulls, their bellies rattled with growls. And above them, the dark circles of gun barrels like empty eye sockets. And Joel had brought them.

Leanne backed up and looked at Casey, her mind fixed on the knife wrapped in a t-shirt at the bottom of her rucksack.

Casey shook her head quickly.

"There's no point in running," a soldier said. "The

dogs are faster than you can ever be, and you'll never outrun a bullet. Best to come without fuss. Then no one gets hurt."

Casey nodded and raised her hands to the sides of her head. "Ok," she said. "Don't hurt anyone. I'm not going to run."

32

The kitchen was typically farmhouse in style, like a picture from one of those interior design magazines Leanne's mum used to read, except that it was neither clean, nor tidy. Her mum had always had grand plans for redecorating their house, but, somehow, it kept dropping down the priority list in favour of something more urgent.

All of the cupboard doors here were matching pine, with small ceramic handles. The large dining table matched, its top rutted and pitted with years of use. Around the table, each wooden chair sported a blue gingham seat cushion, tied to the spindles. On the top of the kitchen cupboards, an array of blue and white jugs were lined up, clearly existing for nothing more than decorative purposes. A copper jelly mould hung on the wall by the oven. Leanne had seen them on Bargain Hunt once, this one was shaped like a fish.

Leanne couldn't imagine why anyone would want fish-shaped jelly.

Leanne was sitting at one end of the table, with Casey a couple of seats away. Casey kept her eyes focussed on the edge of the table, her thumb nail digging away at the wood. Leanne kept her eyes on Joel, trying to burn her way right through his stupid skull. He was purposefully avoiding her gaze, but he could feel it. His bright red ear told her that. A young soldier lounged in the doorway, his rifle leaning against the wall next to him. He yawned and dropped his head against the wooden frame. Clearly, he'd drawn the short straw to end up on babysitting duty.

"I'll never forgive you for this," Leanne finally said, pouring as much venom into her voice as she could. "I can't believe you'd betray me like this."

Joel kept his eyes locked on the table.

Once she'd started, the words poured out of her, and she could do nothing to stop them. Not that she wanted to even try. "I'm your sister, doesn't that mean anything to you? What happened to family loyalty? You're meant to be looking after me. Do you really think that handing me over to the army is being protective? You're meant to keep me safe, not deliver me to the enemy. I'll never forgive you, Joel. Never. As far as I'm concerned, I don't have a brother anymore. So, thank you. Thanks for leaving me utterly alone, without any family at all. That's really protective of you, isn't it? Doing this to a girl who's already lost both of her parents. Thanks Joel. My God, you're such a dick." His eyes flicked in her direction. "Mum and

Dad would be so bloody disappointed in you," she said.

"I did the responsible thing," he muttered. "The grown-up thing."

"You did the selfish thing. And all because you wanted to impress the boys with the big guns. You're not a hero, you know. All you've done is condemn Casey to god-only-knows-what, and I'll never forgive you for it."

"Whatever. I only did what I thought was best, and if you can't see that, maybe you're better off without me anyway. Because I'm sure-as-hell better off without you."

He glanced up as another soldier came into the room. This one was older, and by the way their guard quickly straightened up, Leanne guessed that this was the man in charge.

"I am better off without you," Leanne snapped back. "You're the only reason me and Casey are prisoners now. I hope you're proud of yourself."

The captain patted Joel on the shoulder. "Ignore her. You did the right thing, and that won't be forgotten when we come out the other side of all this."

"So, he's not getting the bounty then?" Leanne said. She looked back at Joel. "Apparently, there's quite a bounty on Casey's head. If you were a real soldier you'd be getting that. Is it still such a sweet deal? Worth losing your sister over?"

"Is there really a bounty?" Joel asked the captain.

"Don't worry, lad, you'll get what's owed to you."

Leanne snorted.

"What's going to happen to the girl?" Joel asked.

"Casey," said Leanne. "Her name is Casey."

"That's up to the scientists," the captain replied. "If she carried some kind of cure, they'll do whatever they need to. For the greater good."

"What do you think they might do to her, Joel?" Leanne asked.

"I don't know," he mumbled in reply.

"Look at her. Look at her! Look at her and have a think about what they might do."

Joel pushed his chair back and pounded out of the room.

The captain stepped over to Leanne. He braced his hands on the table and leaned down to her. "He is all the family you have left. You'll do well to remember that."

"He's the one that needs to remember that. I'm all too aware."

33

Casey still hadn't spoken a single word, or met eyes with anyone, since they'd been brought to the farm. At least she was eating, though. And at least they finally had something better than foil wrapped survival rations.

Leanne tucked into her meal hungrily; she'd had nothing to eat since mid-morning, and it was late now; the sinking sun throwing a deep amber light across the kitchen tiles.

She glanced up at Joel. He appeared to have recovered from his earlier sulking, as he drank beers and shared jokes with the soldiers. It was pathetic; his desperation to be accepted by them, to pretend he was one of them. He wasn't. And as soon as they no longer needed him, they'd leave him behind without a thought. Served him right.

The captain pushed his way back into the

kitchen, and dropped their two rucksacks onto the table. He pulled one open and set about emptying its contents, one item at a time. He made a show of each object, holding it up as if he were auctioning it off, before laying it neatly in front of him. Finally, he pulled out the t-shirt bundle. He weighed it in his hand and raised an eyebrow at Leanne. He unwrapped the knife and placed it down with everything else.

"What happened to Privates Kenton and Dexter?"

Leanne looked at Casey. She continued eating, ignoring the question completely.

"What happened out there?" he asked again. He looked from Leanne to Casey, and back again. "This isn't some little game. You do realise how serious this is? One soldier is dead, and the other is missing."

Casey continued eating. Leanne stared at the knife.

"This is not the time to keep quiet." He sighed. "We know that you didn't do it yourselves, I think we can be certain that two girls didn't remove a soldier's head, but we need to know what happened. Maybe we can still recover Kenton alive." He leaned forward and lowered his voice. "Was it the Edgefear?"

Leanne flinched at the word. So they knew. She shook her head. "No. It was the Ancienteye."

Under the table, Casey kicked Leanne's shin. It was accompanied by a warning look.

The captain frowned. "The Ancienteye? That can't be right. Are you sure it was them?"

"It was self-defence," Casey said quickly. "Dex pointed a gun, threatened to kill them. They had no choice but to protect themselves."

Leanne looked up at Joel. His face was a mask of total confusion. He didn't know. They hadn't told him. Perhaps, now, he'd realise he wasn't one of them.

The captain stood up and laughed. "Well, well, pointing a gun at God, that really was a stupid move." He shrugged. "I guess he got what he deserved. What about Kenton? What happened to him? Was it desertion? Did he run away?"

"They took him," Leanne replied. "The Ancienteye took him because they think he might contain the cure they need."

"Why would they think that?"

"Because the Edgefear have his brother, and they found a possible cure in him. The Ancienteye thought maybe Kenton had it too."

The captain clicked his tongue. "I guess there's not a lot we can do about that, then."

"Does this mean they'll give everyone else back?" a soldier asked.

The captain turned around. "The state they come back in, it might not be the best thing."

"But, maybe things can return to normal again. Go back to how they were. Whether we get everyone back, or not."

The captain clapped his hand on the soldier's back. "Perhaps. Perhaps."

"How long have you known about the monsters?" Leanne asked. "Have you always known?"

The captain made his way out of the kitchen, and several of the soldiers followed.

Leanne's question was left unanswered.

34

Leanne pushed away the hand that was shaking her awake.

"No, Mum," she mumbled.

"Leanne," Joel whispered. "Wake up."

"Joel?" Leanne opened her eyes to a room in darkness, but the moonlight shining through the blue gingham curtains reminded her where she was. She buried her head into the pillow as the familiar pain of realisation ran through her entire body.

"Leanne?" Joel whispered, shaking her shoulder again.

She pushed herself up to sitting. "What do you want, Joel?"

"What's the Edgefear? And the Ancienteye? How do you know all that stuff?"

Leanne sighed. "Do we really need to do this right now?"

"They won't tell me anything."

"Of course they won't, Joel. You're not one of them. You're just some punk kid that did what they wanted because they made you feel important for a little while. You're a total idiot."

Joel looked down at the floor. "Thanks a lot."

"Well, what did you think would happen? They'd give you honorary membership to their club? Issue you with a gun?"

"I don't know."

Leanne moved closer to him, nudging his shoulder with hers. "Oh, Joel. I'm sorry, but you really have been a dick."

He nodded.

"You really want to know everything?"

He shifted, turning to face her. "I really do."

"There's no going back. Once you know, the world will never be the same again. So you have to be sure."

"I'm sure."

"God doesn't exist. At least, not how we've always imagined him. He's not some old, bearded guy floating on a cloud. The Edgefear created us, and the world. The Edgefear are monsters. They live in what they call The Heights."

"Like heaven?"

Leanne shook her head. "I don't think so. You need to abandon the idea of that. The idea of above being good, and below being bad."

"So who are the good ones?"

"Honestly, I don't think there are good ones and

bad ones. It's not as black and white as that. The others are the Ancienteye. They live in The Levels. And the world we live in, they call that the Middle Circle."

"And they're the ones that made everyone disappear?"

"The Edgefear were. The Edgefear and the Ancienteye are dying. There's a disease called the Poisonmarch that's killing them all. The Edgefear took people to see if they could find some kind of cure in them."

"Why would people have the cure?"

"Because we're made from them."

"We're made from monsters? Like, in their image, or something?" He looked down at his body.

"No. I haven't seen the Edgefear, but Casey has. She says they're like tentacled creatures. Maybe like a squid, or an octopus. I dunno."

Leanne couldn't see Joel's face in the darkness, just the shine of his wide eyes. And when he spoke again, there was a tremble in his voice.

"And the Ancienteye?"

"I did meet them. They're... I don't know... more like ethereal beings than monsters."

"What was it like? Meeting them."

"Imagine meeting God, face to face, and being really disappointed with what you see."

"They weren't the good ones, then?"

"There aren't goodies and baddies, Joel. To be honest, I got the impression that the Ancienteye didn't really care. About anything. They even seemed kind of resigned to their own extinction. I wonder if they're just kind of bored with everything. I imagine living forever has got to lose its lustre at some point."

"I guess so."

"Joel," Leanne left his name hanging in the darkness for some time. Neither of them spoke. Joel's breathing sounded thick and heavy, like he was trying to breathe away nausea. "Joel," she said again. "I don't think we're going to see Mum and Dad again."

His breathing stopped for a moment, and then continued. "I don't think so either."

"The Ancienteye said the Edgefear wouldn't stop until they found a cure. But they don't care about us, none of them do. We're just entertainment. Entertainment that I get the feeling has become a little boring."

"And even if they do come back..." He took a deep breath. "They showed me a zom, I saw what they're like. They said that's what you were with, that's what Casey was. I honestly thought you were going to die. I didn't know that Casey was fine. I thought she was a zom, just like that one."

"They lied to you. They knew she wasn't like that. That's why they were looking for her, because they think she holds the key to a cure. I guess everyone's looking for cures now."

"It seems they didn't tell me a lot of stuff. I'd heard them mention Edgefear and Ancienteye, I heard those words a lot, Poisonmarch too. But I'd assumed they were military code names. I had no idea that..."

"That everything we'd ever believed, ever been told, was wrong?" Leanne suggested.

"Yeah, that." He leant forward, elbows balanced on his knees, and dropped his head down. "They made me feel like I was a hero, like I was saving the world. They said that I was one of them, fighting the fight for mankind. But they were lying to me the whole time. They used me." He looked up at her. "I'm really sorry, Lea."

She leant over and wrapped her arms around him, dropping her cheek to his shoulder. After a while, his hand came up and gripped the back of her jumper. She realised how much she'd missed this, just this proximity with another person. Breathing against one another, the comfort of his warmth against hers. She drew back, one of her hands resting on his forearm. It wasn't just the heart that got lonely, or the mind or soul, or whatever that essence of people was, but bodies got lonely too. Hugs, kisses, touches. Skin needed skin. Arms needed arms.

As a family, they hadn't ever been particularly touchy-feely, and she'd probably hugged Joel more in the last two years, than in all of their lives prior to that. But it was just the simple proximity she missed. Her dad tousling her hair in the morning, her mum grabbing her wrist to force a quick peck onto her cheek. Walking to school arm in arm with Sophie. Even Joel's play-fighting. All those things that had meant nothing at the time.

"I'll make everything right," Joel said. He shook his head. "All I ever wanted was to protect you, to be a good big brother, but I've managed to screw it all up."

"It's ok, you haven't screwed it all up. You did do a good job, I just couldn't see it. You were right about joining The Arcane. You kept me safe, you kept the power on at home, food coming in. We'd never have survived without you doing what you did. You were right, I was just being selfish and stubborn."

"Me and Dad had an argument. That morning. The day they disappeared. Dad said that I was a waste of space who would never amount to anything. He was right."

"No, he wasn't, and he wouldn't have meant that. People never mean what they say when they're angry. What were you arguing about?"

"I told Dad that I'd dropped out of college."

"You dropped out? Why?"

"I was failing anyway, and I figured I'd rather leave than fail."

"You could have turned it around, you shouldn't have just given up."

He sighed. "It's alright for you, you're the smart one, you always have been. I'm just the disappointing child."

"Dad was really proud of you."

Joel huffed. "I was only doing Sports Science and Business. That's what people do when they don't really know what to do with their lives. Dad was right. I've got no direction, and I was even failing at that."

"Dad was really proud when you started college."

"No, he wasn't. I only went to college so that I didn't have to get a job, everyone knew it."

"You're wrong. I heard Dad boasting about you to Mr Hendricks, more than once. He was so proud of you."

Joel sniffed and rubbed at his nose. "All I've ever wanted is to make Mum and Dad proud of me, like they always were of you, but I just keep screwing it up."

Leanne laid her hand on his, which was tightly balled into a fist. "You did look after me, really well. These guys lied to you, and that's not your fault, but now you have a chance to put things right. Can you drive?"

"Yeah. The Arcane taught me."

"Do you know where Casey is?"

"Yeah, in the basement."

"Do you think you can get rid of whoever's guarding her?"

"Yeah," Leanne could hear the smile in his voice. "Yeah, I know who it is, and I know exactly how to get rid of him. I guess he drew the short straw getting that job, or, more likely, had it given to him. He's one of the young ones, and he is not very good at holding his beer. I've already seen him have a couple of bottles tonight. If he hasn't passed out already, it shouldn't take too much more to do it."

"I doubt it'll be that easy. These men are trained soldiers."

Joel laughed. "I've been with them a good few days now, and, I can tell you, all these guys are is a handful of power-hungry officers leading a load of rookies who are only still taking orders because they're not smart enough to think for themselves. All the smart ones left when their wages stopped coming in. Probably took a handful of guns with them, too. That was the smart move. These guys aren't even organised, they're not even united. There's different groups of army all over the country, all with different ideas about how things should be done. They're fighting against each other more than the zoms. They were telling me; they've lost more men to friendly fire, or not so friendly as it turns out, than they have to anything else."

Leanne nodded. "Ok. I trust you. Let's get it done."

The house was still as they crept down the stairs, the air filled with a symphony of snores and grunts. The intoxicated sleep of men. Leanne could only hope that it was enough to keep them unconscious, as every single stair erupted with its own concerto of creaks and cracks.

When they reached the hallway, and Leanne stepped onto the stone tiles, she realised she'd been holding her breath through the whole descent.

Joel peeked into the kitchen, raising his thumb to Leanne. He gestured for her to wait in the doorway, while he collected some beer bottles from the fridge. They jangled together merrily, as if they saw a funny side to all of this that Leanne couldn't appreciate.

Joel led Leanne down the hallway, to a small

room that appeared to be serving as a pantry and cloakroom simultaneously. Food was stacked haphazardly amongst hats and gloves, while boots crowded together under the counter.

Joel hadn't been wrong, either; the young soldier was slumped in a chair next to the basement door, his eyes heavy, his head lolling. He looked up and gave Joel a lazy smile.

"Alright, mate?" he said.

Joel shrugged. "Couldn't sleep. Have you got any cigarettes?"

The soldier patted down his pockets until he found what he was looking for. He grinned and held out a crumpled packet.

Joel lifted the bottles, demonstrating that he had no free hands.

"Let me lighten your load there," the soldier said, taking a beer from him.

Joel handed a beer to Leanne, and opened the last one for himself. "Coming for a smoke?"

"I shouldn't," said the soldier, nodding towards the basement.

"C'mon, what's she gonna do? Unbolt it from the inside?"

The soldier shrugged and struggled to his feet, almost falling twice before it made it to being upright. He followed them out into the crisp, cool night air.

A large moon sat high in the sky, not quite full, slightly deflated on one side. The stars swept across the darkness like spilt glitter; not just individual twinkling stars, but rivers of them, that flowed with hues of purple and blue. Leanne gazed at it; she'd rarely seen the sky without the glare of street lights erasing it into a sickly orange. In fact, she'd rarely ever looked up. Humans didn't, did they? And, despite knowing the truth, she almost found herself believing that she was looking straight into heaven.

Turning around, she took in more of the sky, her eyes hungrily demanding extra portions of it. She took a few paces back, reducing the amount of sky the farmhouse blocked from view.

"Jesus!" she cried, her knees faltering. She managed to stay on her feet, but only just.

"What is it?" Joel walked to meet her, and followed the line of her gaze.

The rip was far wider than it had been; the mouth had opened, and light flowed through it. Dark light, if that were possible. Deep red and brown, smudged into the darkness of the night as if a hand had been dragged across those lips.

Joel gripped Leanne's arm, steadying himself. "What the hell is that?"

"Bloody hell," said the soldier, joining them. "That's got bigger."

"What is it?" Joel asked again.

"The rip. We're guessing it's a doorway of sorts. Between our world, and theirs."

"The Middle Circle and the Heights," Leanne whispered.

"Is something... Is something coming through that?" Joel asked.

"Sooner or later," the soldier replied. "Perhaps

sooner now." He took a long swig of beer. "Screw this," he said, and emptied his bottle into his mouth. "Are you drinking that?" He gestured towards Leanne's drink. She relinquished the bottle happily. The soldier emptied it. "Shit," he said. "Shitting shit." He sat down on the ground, his torso swaying from side to side.

Leanne stood and stared up at the rip.

"Are the Edgefear coming through that?" Joel whispered.

"I dunno, maybe."

"Or the zoms."

"The Poisonmarch." Leanne turned to Joel. "I wonder how many other people are staring up at it every night. People who have no idea what might come through there."

"It's probably better not to know. I'm pretty sure knowing what's on the other side of that isn't bringing me any comfort." He leant forward, his hands braced against his knees, as if he were about to retch. "Bloody hell."

"Well, it worked." Leanne pointed down at the soldier. He was lying on the floor now, his knees tucked into his stomach. Fetal.

Joel gently nudged him with his foot. He didn't stir. "Let's get Casey."

"I'll get Casey. You see if any of these Land Rovers have keys in them."

As Leanne drew back the bolt on the basement door, she gently called through the wooden panels. "It's Leanne. We're busting you out." She didn't want to step in without announcing herself, only to find Casey acting out her own escape plan by hitting her over the head with something heavy.

Casey was waiting on the other side, halfway up the basement steps. She quickly glanced down into the darkness below her. "Let's get out of here."

Hand in hand, they ran back into the cool night air, and spotted Joel madly waving from the driving seat of a truck. They ran around the far side of it, clambering in next to him.

They all winced as the engine roared, but if anyone woke up now, they'd never get outside in time to stop them.

"Go!" Leanne shouted, and the vehicle jumped forward, the engine cutting out. "What's happened?"

"Sorry, I stalled it. Let me try again. Sorry."

He turned the engine off, muttering to himself as he ran through the process of restarting it. Leanne jammed her fists against her thighs, trying not to scream at him to hurry up.

The engine roared again, and the truck lurched forward, but this time, the engine continued, and they slowly pulled out of the yard, picking up speed as they hit the farm track. The Land Rover jumped and bounced over the dried, rutted earth, and Leanne pulled her seatbelt across her, urging Casey to do the same.

Joel grinned at her. "Safety first." He hooked his thumb behind the belt already laid across his chest.

When they heard the first crack of gunfire, Leanne thought it was the truck, hitting a rock, or backfiring. But when the crackle continued, and the back window shattered, there was no passing it off as something harmless.

"They're shooting at us!" Joel yelled. "Get down!"

Leanne tucked her head below the back of the seat, and pushed Casey down with her.

"I can't believe they're shooting at us," Casey cried.

"I can," replied Joel, spinning the steering wheel. But then it was spinning the other way, and his hands simply skidded across it. "Hold on!" he screamed, raising his own arms up to cover his face.

The truck bounced, and it felt like an age passed before it landed again. But it didn't land upright, and the impact threw it onto its side. Leanne's head snapped back and forth as the vehicle tumbled. The world around them spun out of control, and they were flipped around like toys. Her head hit something hard, and a bright flash of pain shot through her vision, blocking out everything else. And then they were still. The vehicle on one side. And Leanne could feel the warmth of blood flowing down one side of her face. She tried to raise her hand to it, but it wouldn't respond. She blinked, but saw only blackness. And she smelt the stench of petrol, and felt heat on the back of her neck. She heard Casey whimper next to her, but Joel was silent. The heat flared, and then there was cold air, and hands, and voices. She tried to fight, but her strength was gone. Hands grabbed, and pulled, and everything went quiet.

35

It was white. Everything was white. And then there was blue. A stripe of blue. And the shine of chrome. Leanne closed her eyes again. It was too much at once. She worked through the senses one at a time. Softness surrounded her, against her skin. Her mouth was dry, a slight metallic taste on the side of her tongue. She could smell cleaning fluids. Bleach. Wherever she was, it was quiet, but she could hear breathing. Her own? She held her breath. No. Someone was sleeping, their breaths deep and long.

Only then, did she try opening her eyes again. She gradually revealed the world through the filter of her eyelashes. White. Again. Achingly white. Sterile. That was the word that came into her mind. Sterile. A hospital.

She turned her stiff, aching neck to one side. In the bed beside her, Joel was sleeping. He was on his side, turned away from her, but she knew it was him. She'd stared at the back of his head enough times in her life to recognise him from it. He had turned calling 'shotgun' into a complicated challenge that he always won. Forever adding rules that Leanne was held to, but he was immune from. She'd spent many car journeys incarcerated in the back seat, staring at the back of that head, willing it to explode.

She began mentally working her way up her body. Toes. Still wriggled. Knees. Still functional. Buttocks. Still clenchable. She wriggled her fingers. Bent her elbows. Hunched her shoulders. And whimpered at the pain. That's where she was hurt. Her right shoulder. She slowly lifted her left arm and touched her skin. No bandage. She was in one piece. She was lucky. She wondered if Joel had been equally fortunate. Or Casey. Casey. If they were in hospital, that means they had her.

She attempted to sit, but the pain that coursed through her skull and her shoulder forced her back down. She wasn't going anywhere. She couldn't do anything to help Casey in this state.

"Joel," she hissed. He didn't stir. "Joel." Louder this time, but his breathing kept its same, regular rhythm. "Joel!"

With a groan, he rolled over to face her, jamming the heels of his hands deep into his eyes.

"You're awake then," he said.

"Yeah, I'm awake. Are you ok?"

"Pretty much. Bumps, bruises, a couple of broken fingers." He held up his right hand, showing two swollen digits taped together.

"I've done something to my shoulder," Leanne said. "It really hurts."

"It's separated, they said. You've also got a nasty gash on your head, and concussion. But, to be honest, we're all really lucky."

Leanne nodded. "Is there any water?"

"Yeah, I'll get it for you." He sat up and poured a glass from the jug on the bedside table between them. He popped a straw into it. "You shouldn't try to sit up." He smiled weakly as he perched on the edge of her bed, and lifted the glass so that she could reach the straw.

"Thank you. You're a good nursemaid."

"I can at least try to do something right."

"It wasn't your fault. They were shooting at us."

He shrugged. "Maybe if I was a better driver, or if I hadn't stalled it... I guess I screwed up again, huh?"

"Don't you dare say that. What you did, it was really brave, Joel. I'm really proud of you. And Mum and Dad would be too. This was not your fault."

He sighed. "They took Casey."

"She's still alive, at least."

"Hopefully. What do you think they'll do to her?"

"Probably just take her blood. Don't worry, as long as she's the only person who's recovered from the Poisonmarch, they have to keep her alive. Otherwise they lose all hope of finding a cure."

"I hope you're right." He held up his hand. "Because we won't be attempting any more daring escapes for a while."

Leanne laughed carefully, trying not to jolt her body too much. "That's true. Where are we, anyway?"

"I'm not sure. A hospital somewhere. Maybe even a military hospital. Could be anywhere in the country though."

"What day is it now?"

Joel looked around the small room. "I don't even know what time it is. There are no windows. No dark or light."

"That might be a good thing, I'm not sure I'm ready to see the night sky again just yet."

Joel looked down at the floor for a moment, his face screwed into a frown. "I'm glad you're ok," he finally said. "I mean, I was really worried about you. I was scared."

"It's ok. You can say it."

He looked at her. "What?"

"I. Love. You." She separated the words out, taunting him.

He turned away. "Shut up. I just didn't want you on my conscience."

"You don't need to say it. I know you love your little sister with all your heart."

"Watch it, or I'll separate your other shoulder." He stood up and looked down at her. "Just concentrate on mending. There's nothing we can do about Casey right now."

Someone tapped gently on the door, and Joel hopped back onto his bed, legs crossed.

A man came in, dressed in a white jacket, a tray of food and drink in his hands. He crossed the room slowly, awkwardly, not used to balancing meals on trays.

He smiled apologetically at the floor between the beds, shrugging one shoulder.

"Sorry, it's nothing fancy," he said. "The facilities here aren't really gourmet."

He handed Leanne a plate topped with a plastic-wrapped sandwich, and a packet of crisps. As he did so, the crisps slipped off and into her lap. "Sorry," he winced.

He placed the tray on the bedside table, and handed Leanne a bottle of water. Joel took his offerings from the tray himself.

"Better than nothing, I suppose," said Joel. "Any chance of a side order of answers? Where are we? What the hell is this place? What's going to happen to us? How long are you going to keep us here?"

The man backed away, ducking his head, and slightly raising his hands. "I'm not supposed to talk to you."

"Not supposed to talk to us? We deserve some answers. We're being held against our will, and we don't even know whereabouts in the country we are. If we even are still in England."

"They wouldn't have taken us abroad," Leanne said quietly.

"You don't know that," Joel snapped, keeping his gaze on the man. "Tell us where we are."

"I can't tell you anything. I'm sorry. It's my only order. Well... that, and, not to let you die. If I can help it." His eyes flicked up and caught Leanne's gaze. He smiled quickly, just a flash of a grin, before returning his focus to the floor.

"Well, thank you," said Leanne. "We appreciate you looking after us."

"Don't be too grateful, I'm actually a healthcare scientist in clinical biochemistry." He raised his eyes to Leanne, but kept his chin lowered, peering at her from under his pale eyebrows.

"What does that mean?" she asked.

He gave a small shrug. "It basically means that I'm not a doctor in the way that you'd like me to be. That you need me to be."

"I'm sure you're doing a great job. Can you tell me how long my shoulder will take to get better?"

"You should be fully recovered in three to four weeks. Certainly no more than eight. As long as you rest it properly, and complete any rehabilitation advice. Not that I can give you any expert advice. So, no more escape attempts." He tried wagging a finger at her, but his shyness got the better of him, and the gesture withered away.

She laughed politely. "You needn't worry about that, we have nothing planned."

He grinned. "That's good to hear."

"What's your name?"

"Mick. And you're Leanne." He blushed, clearing his throat to try and cover it.

"That's right. Mick, do you know anything about Casey?"

He shifted his weight and rubbed at the back of one hand. He glanced quickly towards the door. "I don't have any information," he said, running the words into one another.

"Mick, can you at least tell us if she's safe? Or if she's still alive? She means a lot to me. I'd be really grateful."

He nodded once. "Yes, she's still alive."

Leanne exhaled. "Is she going to be ok?"

He raised a hand and tugged at the skin at the front of his neck. His gaze returned to the floor. "I don't know," he said at last.

"But, you must know something."

He shook his head and looked back up at her. "I'm down here serving sandwiches and drinks. Do you really think I'm high up in the decision making process?" He held her gaze for a moment, before waving a hand in resignation. "I'd better be going."

He turned hesitantly, his body stuttering in the motion, the decision to leave not quite finalised. But Leanne didn't get to see what course of action he finally settled on; the lights clicked off, and the room was swallowed up by complete and unbroken darkness.

Leanne blinked. She lifted her hand in front of her face, but, with no windows in the room, the blackness was deep and engulfing. It had drowned out everything, blanketed the world, erased all vision. It danced and squirmed in front of her as her brain attempted to process some kind of sense, to correct the blind spot.

"Don't worry," came Mick's voice, tiny and unsure. "It'll be a problem with the generator, the emergency lights will come on in a second."

As the words left his mouth, the room was bathed in a vile green glow. Above the door, the exit sign illuminated; the stick man running for freedom.

Leanne looked over at Joel, who was still sitting, cross-legged, on his bed. He looked back at her, his face highlighted in lime.

"Just stay put," Mick said. "I'll check out what's happening." For a moment, he didn't move, but when he did, he went quickly. Not determinedly, though, not striding with purpose. More of a hurried shuffle to take him across the room before he changed his mind again.

"Were you flirting with him?" hissed Joel.

Leanne snapped her head round to him, pain shooting up through her shoulder. "Really, Joel?"

"We appreciate you looking after us." He mimicked her, dancing his hands around idiotically.

She looked over at Mick, who had reached the door. He pulled it open with some difficulty; it was heavy for his slight frame. A soldier was standing outside. Armed.

"What's happening?" asked Mick.

"I don't know," said the soldier defensively. He turned away from Mick, as if his reply was decisive, and the conversation finished.

"Can you go and find out?"

"My orders are to stay put."

"What the hell do you think these kids are going to do right now?" His voice squeaked as he raised it, and it was barely any louder than before. He leaned forward, whispering something to the soldier that Leanne couldn't hear.

The soldier sighed loudly. "Fine. But don't let them out of the room."

Mick let the door drop shut. For a moment, he just stood there, one hand still raised towards the handle. He stared down at the floor. After taking a deep breath, he turned back around.

"I'm sure that the generator will be up and running again soon."

"Mick," Leanne said. "Will you be straight with us? We know about the Edgefear, and the Ancienteye, and Poisonmarch. We know everything. Please, tell us what's really going on."

Mick walked slowly back towards them, his bottom lip held between his teeth. He shook his head.

"Just tell us!" yelled Joel. His voice bounced around the room, hitting Mick over and over.

Slowly, Mick sank to his knees. He took a deep breath.

"We kept you all sedated for three days, during which that rip in the sky, that mouth, opened up. The army had expected one of two things: either billions of zoms coming through to decimate us, or the Edgefear. Neither were particularly pleasant scenarios, but the Edgefear came up with something far, far worse. The Edgefear gave the people back, everyone they'd taken, all five billion and whatever of them, but they dropped them from the goddamn sky. It was raining people. Living, fully conscious people." He reached his hands forward, palms upwards, as if he were trying to catch them. His shoulders shook, the shudder passing through his whole body, and it didn't stop. "We went out to see—of course we bloody did—someone tells you what's happening, and how can you believe something like that? How can you even imagine it without seeing it for yourself?" He reached his hands further forward, curling in on himself. "She fell right in front of me. Inches away. She screamed all the way down, and then, she just stopped." He sat up and wiped his hands on his jacket, his face twisted. "She was a tiny child, three or four years old, and..." Tears began to come down his cheeks, dripping from the base of his chin. "Oh God, and there were babies, there were babies taken."

He curled back up, his sobs turning into tortured wails. But no screams were adequate here. No tearing at clothes, or hair, or skin, nothing would ever be enough to adequately express or expel the horror. The grief. The absolute inconceivable madness.

The shudder that overtook Leanne started in the core of her heart. She would always be convinced of that. Her heart felt as if it were turning itself inside out, and then her other organs followed suit. Her entire body spasmed and shook with grief. But that word didn't come anywhere close to what it needed to be. She didn't have a word for this. Humans didn't have a word for this. How could they? How could they have possibly had a word for this?

Joel slowly climbed from his bed. He looked down at Mick, and hesitated, as if considering going to him, comforting him. But there would be no comforting this. No healing of this. This was a wound that would gape for generations. Bloody, raw, unhealing. The skin shredded and unable to be stitched.

Joel turned to Leanne and took her hand in his.

"Mum and Dad," Leanne whispered.

"I know." Joel sank to his knees, just as Mick had, and drew Leanne's hand to his forehead. They wept without holding back, howling, and Leanne thought that they would never be able to stop.

36

The door swung open, bouncing to the furthest extent of its hinges. In just a few strides, the soldier was across the room, roughly grabbing Mick by the arm, and wrenching him to his feet.

Mick's face was streaked with tears, and he dragged his sleeves across it unabashedly.

"We're in lockdown," the soldier said. "No one in. No one out." As he spoke, his body twitched and fidgeted. Full of excess energy, like a child after too much sugar. Desperate to run, but with nowhere to run to. He turned to Joel and Leanne, jabbing a finger at them. "You guys are lucky you're stuck in here. Seriously, thank your lucky stars." He shook his head. "Screw protocol, screw orders. The Edgefear have come through, and they're hell-bent on taking everyone down with them. They're dying, literally dropping down dead, as they're pulling the world apart. They're done for, and they are pissed. Screw this shit."

"What do you mean?" Leanne asked. "What's happening up there? And what are you guys doing about it?"

"What are we supposed to do about it? Some guys are up there, trying to fight back, but how, exactly, do you fight a monster? Or a God? Or whatever the hell they are? It's every man for himself now. Save your own damn souls."

He retraced the few strides that had brought him across the room, and then he was gone, the door dropping closed behind him.

Leanne looked from Joel, to Mick, and back again. Like reflections, they did the same.

"What do we do now?" Joel ventured. But how was there an answer to that?

Mick rubbed at his face again, rubbing away tears with the heels of his hands. He gave his head a shake. "You heard him. No one in. No one out. We're best off here, anyway. We're in a secure, underground bunker. We couldn't possibly find anywhere safer to be."

"So, we just hide down here and let whatever happens happen?" Leanne asked.

"What do you want to do?" squealed Mick. "You're just a girl. If the army can't do anything, what exactly do you expect to do?" He dropped his arms heavily to his sides. His head went with them, his chin dropping to his chest. He took a deep breath. "If the Edgefear are dying, this is all going to be over soon. It makes sense to just stay here and wait it out."

"Mick? Will you put my arm in a sling so that I can get up? I need to go and find Casey."

"They're not going to let you just wander in for a chat," said Joel.

"The place will be in chaos. What harm will it do to see how far we can get?"

"Harm to you. You're meant to be resting your shoulder."

"He's right," said Mick.

"Casey's just a kid, and she's going to be terrified. Besides, they don't even need her anymore. Everyone who was infected with Poisonmarch is dead. They've probably just left her to fend for herself. Mick. Will you put my arm in a sling, please? I'm going to look for her whether you do it or not."

Joel stepped down to the floor and came over to Leanne's bed, looking down at her. "Why does Casey matter so much to you? You didn't even know her before all this."

"If we let Casey die, then everything has been for nothing, and we may as well give up on hope altogether. Wouldn't you have taken better care of your childhood if you'd known that it would end like this?"

"What are you talking about? That doesn't make any sense."

"It doesn't have to," she snapped. "Does anything in this world make sense anymore?"

Joel nodded and gave Leanne half a smile. He looked up at Mick who crossed to the cupboards in the corner, and set about searching through them.

"Can you help me stand up, Joel?"

With every movement, pain ran through her shoulder, stretching its thorns up her neck, into her skull, pricking the back of her eyes. The brambles of pain reached down her arms, snagging each of her fingers.

Mick came over with a sling. Gently taking her hand, he lifted her arm and laid it up against her chest, her fingers touching her good shoulder. She closed her eyes against the sting of tears, a whimper escaping her throat.

"Sorry," whispered Mick.

"It's ok," she whispered back.

"Would you like some pain relief?"

"No, thank you. I want to stay sharp."

"It's just some painkillers."

"No, I'm fine." She smiled at Joel, before turning back to Mick. "Will you show us where Casey is?"

He nodded. "Let's go."

The corridors were lit in the same sickly green, a strip of emergency lighting running along the ceiling. It was eerily quiet and still. Leanne had expected people running around, screaming. Panic. She realised they had gone beyond that. The bunker was deep in an atmosphere of fatalistic acceptance. It had given up. Resigned itself to whatever might happen to it. Somewhere, a long way off, they heard shouting. Above them, something like thunder rumbled deeply, its voice carrying down through the walls. Now and again, they passed an open door and heard someone sobbing beyond it. Otherwise, it was as if they were the last people alive.

"Here we are," said Mick, turning off the corridor. They stepped into a large laboratory, the computers on each desk humming contentedly to themselves, awaiting the return of whoever had been with them.

"Where did everyone go?" whispered Leanne.

"I don't know," Mick replied.

At the end of the room, a glass wall separated out a room; a cell. Inside, Casey was lying on a bed, her back turned to them, her knees scrunched up to her chest.

"Casey!" cried out Leanne, knocking on the glass partition. Casey didn't move.

"Soundproof," Mick said. He stepped to one side, and pressed a button on a small intercom box, nodding at Leanne.

"Casey?" she said.

In a single motion, Casey was off the bed, and up against the glass. With both hands raised, she slammed them repeatedly against the partition, her mouth gaping with words Leanne couldn't hear.

"Can we let her out?" Leanne asked Mick.

He bent, and pushed a code into the keypad of the intercom. The door slid open. Casey practically tumbled out of the room, her trainers squeaking on the floor as she rounded the corner. She skidded to a stop in front of Leanne, arms raised, ready to throw herself against her. She looked the sling, and contented to simply grab hold of Leanne's free hand, squeezing it tightly.

"What happened? Are you ok?"

Leanne nodded, her throat too full of tears to speak.

"You came for me," Casey said. "You really came."

Leanne nodded again, swallowing hard. "I could never leave you," she whispered. "Are you ok? Have they hurt you?"

She shook her head. "Just a few needle pricks. I'm alright." She glanced at Joel, giving him a quick nod. "It's ok. I forgive you. You didn't know."

"Thanks," said Joel, looking down at his shoes.

"I thought I was going to be stuck here forever after everyone left. They just ran. No one thought about me locked in there."

"Where do you run to when monsters are attacking the whole planet?" Leanne asked.

Casey smiled and shook her head.

"It doesn't matter," said Joel. "You just run. Anywhere. It's just the fight or flight reflex kicking in. Can't you feel it? Your legs tingling?"

Leanne nodded. "I guess so. Like restlessness, or nervous energy. We're just biology, I suppose, at the end of the day."

Joel stepped forward and placed his hand on top of Casey's, which still held onto Leanne.

"But it doesn't make our connections less important," he said. "We're just animals, when it comes down to it, but this is real too. Friendship. Family. Love. All of it matters. And we have to look after it." He looked up. "And not let them take it away from us."

They all ducked as the sky above them cracked, the sound more than thunder, more than gunfire. It sounded like the world itself were being split open. The emergency lights flickered, and went out.

"Don't let go," Leanne whispered. She felt Casey and Joel tighten their grip.

"What's happening?" Casey asked.

The crack came again, accompanied this time with creaking, the squeal of metal buckling, the tang-tang-tang of wires breaking. Light rushed into the room, grabbing their eyes, blocking out everything else. Leanne screwed hers shut, turning her head away from the brightness.

Casey screamed, wrenching her hand free. She ran, dropping to her knees mid-stride, sliding under a desk, disappearing.

Joel looked at Leanne, his eyes wide. He tipped his head back, staring up at the open sky above them. He said something, but Leanne couldn't hear him properly. It might have been "This is it," but Leanne wasn't certain. She may have listened closer if she had known it would be the last words he ever said to her.

When the tentacle reached down, and wrapped around his waist, he looked shocked at first. And then he smiled at Leanne. It wasn't a fearful smile, a smile to cover his terror, or to comfort her. It was peaceful, serene even, as if everything was exactly as it should be. As if he had known this would happen, as if it were the only way things could have ended. His hand left hers, and he was flung into the sky.

"No!" Leanne wailed, dropping to the floor. A sharp pain clawed at her shoulder, but it paled against the anguish that tore through her insides. "No!" She pounded her fist into her thigh, wishing that she could pound her entire body into dust. "No!"

The world was gone. It was over. It was done. And Leanne was empty. Her body was a void, a vacuum, an endless darkness. She was filled only with a throbbing ache of torment. What else was left for her to feel? She would be alone until she died, and she would never feel another thing. And that was how it should be. It was what they deserved. She would honour them by devoting her life to this pain. This is what they deserved. Her life. She gasped as her body filled with tears that refused to leave her, that were too thick, too solid to squeeze from her eyes.

She allowed the hands to take hold of her, to lift her to her feet. They turned her around, and the arms enveloped her.

But the body against hers wasn't warm. The chest didn't rise and fall with hers. It was smooth, still, and cool. She pulled away.

"It is over," the Ancienteye said.

Leanne stared at it. At its disgusting form that wavered, that never quite managed to solidify.

"Now? Now?" she said. "Now you turn up? After the Edgefear have destroyed everything? Where were you hiding?" Her body was rigid, as if she had hold of a live electric cable.

The Ancienteye held out its hands. "What should we have done?"

"Saved us. Saved the world. Saved Joel."

"The Edgefear created their toy and, like a spoilt child, it destroyed it too."

"Their 'toy' was living, and breathing, and feeling. Their 'toy' loved this world and loved the people it took away. Tell me why I shouldn't kill you right now."

"What would be the point? I am dying, and I am the very last of my kind."

"Good. I hope it hurts like hell."

The Ancienteye lowered its gaze and gestured towards Casey. "You're safe," it said. "You're safe."

Casey crawled out from under the table, and stood in front of the Ancienteye, her head bowed. "Yes," she said.

"Are you unharmed?"

"Yes."

"Why does she matter?" demanded Leanne. "Why care about her?"

"Because she is our only hope," replied the Ancienteye. "When the Edgefear gave us Casey, we made her our insurance. She is the secret to our long-term survival."

"How?"

"She carries our..." it searched for the right word. "Blueprint. Our design. She carries the building blocks to recreate us."

"I do?" Casey looked down at herself, as if she might see the plans drawn onto her skin.

"You carry our future within you."

Leanne pushed Casey aside. "You do not have a future. You're done. You're dead. And this world is far better off without you."

The Ancienteye nodded. "That may well be, but the fight to survive is an instinct. The Edgefear went out fighting. This is our fight."

"And, how does this blueprint help you? Is an Ancienteye going to burst out of her stomach? Have you impregnated her?"

"The technology and knowledge to recreate us doesn't yet exist. But humans are resourceful, and inventive, and, in time, they will be able to recreate us from what we have placed inside her."

"Why would we?"

"Maybe you won't. But humans are also curious, and boastful. Humans would resurrect us simply to prove that they can."

"What happens if she dies before we find out how? Then you'll be gone forever."

The Ancienteye nodded. "Casey will live a long, long life. There's no way of knowing how long. Hundreds, perhaps thousands of years. She will never get sick, and she will age far slower than other humans. Any children she has will also carry the blueprint, and enjoy extended life."

"Enjoy?" Leanne stepped closer to the Ancienteye. "You and your monster friends got so bored you created a world to entertain you. And you expect Casey to enjoy the life you've given her?" She grabbed Casey's wrist and dragged her forward.

"Everyone she loves is gone. Everyone she ever loves will die. This isn't some kind of gift you've given her, it's a curse. You've condemned her to thousands of years alone. You're alone now. The last of your kind. How does that feel?" She clenched and unclenched her shaking hands.

"We all have our burdens."

Leanne scoffed, turning away from the creature. She looked at Casey, and the decision was easy. It wasn't even a choice.

"Put it into me, too," she said. "Put your blueprint into me."

"I cannot."

"Do it! You, and them—" she gestured wildly towards the sky "—have taken everyone away from me. You've left me completely alone in the world, except for Casey. And she is completely alone, except for me. Before you die, do one decent thing. Do one thing to actually make someone else's life better. Do one thing that actually matters, that makes a difference. Put your damn blueprint in me too."

The Ancienteye lifted his hands, and looked at them. "I don't know that I have time."

"Then do it now."

37

Leanne drew back the net curtain and looked out at the street beyond. The same street she'd looked at for years. But it was different now, the whole world was different. On the horizon, she could see the lazy stream of smoke rising into the clouds. The government had decided to burn the bodies, in case the Poisonmarch virus spread. The line of smoke had been a constant for months; a pyre that burnt continually. A reminder. A marker. A memorial. People had taken to facing that way to pray. Those who didn't know all of the Gods were dead. Or those who still found comfort in the act, despite there being no one left to hear them.

She dropped the curtain back and turned to the living room she'd grown up in. The TV was turned down low, the new prime minister was making a rousing speech about how it was time to look forward, to get back to work, and build a new future for ourselves. He deftly skipped around the issue of repopulating the planet, managing to imply that it was the duty of the women to pop out as many babies as they could, without actually saying it.

When the first TV channel had returned, it had been almost like magic, like it was the first time anyone had seen anything like it. People had huddled into takeaways, leaning on the counter, staring up at the TV like it was some kind of miracle. They congregated into single houses, holding hands as they watched the very first broadcast since everything had happened. There were still only three channels to choose from, and they largely showed the same programmes. One had tried playing old reruns of shows from before, but it only served to drive home everything that we had lost, and the government instructed it to stop. The broadcasters were closely monitored, allowed only to make programmes that looked to the future, that inspired hope.

Leanne looked up as Casey came into the room.

"What's he nattering about today?" she asked, nodding towards the TV.

"Who cares?" Leanne switched it off. "I wonder how many prime ministers we'll see in our lifetimes. Suddenly, a five-year term seems like the blink of an eye, doesn't it?"

Casey smiled. So much went unsaid between them now. They could almost feel one another's thoughts.

"What are you going to do today?" Casey asked

her.

Leanne nudged her bag with her foot. "I am going back to school."

"It's open again?"

"Finally. I never imagined I could get bored of school holidays, but I'm actually really excited to go back."

"I suppose we'll get bored of a lot of things."

"Let's just hope the world changes quickly enough to keep us interested."

Casey nodded. "Then let's start today. I guess I'd better come with you."

"You should. School will become compulsory again soon enough. And the world will start to look like it used to."

"Just a lot emptier."

There were less than one billion people left on the planet, and nature was reclaiming abandoned towns as people flocked together. The government had, originally, tried to bring everyone to London. But people were too attached to their homes. Those whose homes hadn't been destroyed by the Edgefear, of course. They wanted to stay where things were familiar. Where they could find some comfort in the familiarity. Though they also wanted to be together, to create communities, tribes. And so, there were pockets of people all over the country, separated by vast distances of nothing. Of empty roads and empty towns, and nature pushing its way up through the tarmac.

Leanne cocked her head towards the front door.

"Come on then, lets get started on our own future."

Casey laughed. "Yeah, and life's too short, right?"

Leanne swung her bag onto her shoulder, and glanced around the living room. "See you later," she whispered to her parents, to Joel. The ghosts of them were here, and she would always carry them with her. But she had a lot of years ahead of her, and many more ghosts to pick up along the way. "Is it crazy to still believe in heaven?" she asked out loud.

"All of this is crazy," said Casey. "But it's our crazy."

Leanne pulled Casey into her and kissed the top of her head. "Then, let's embrace this crazy world and make it ours. Our 'new normal'."

They pulled on their issued face masks before stepping outside. The wearing of them was law now, but they did offer relief from the constant scent of burning flesh and hair.

Leanne stopped and looked at Mr Hendricks' house. One side of it had been torn open, like a doll house with the wall opening on a hinge. His daughters' bedroom, and the kitchen below, opened up to the world like a wound.

Casey stopped next to her and followed her gaze. "What do you think happened to him?"

"I have no idea. I just hope that he found some kind of peace. Somehow." She turned back to the street and carried on down the path. "I convinced Neil to come and teach at the school," she said. "He doesn't exactly have anything else to do."

"That's good. He's nice. I think he'll make a good

teacher. He helped a lot of people by holding funerals, even if there weren't any bodies to actually bury."

"Yes. Giving people a chance to say a proper goodbye. That was important. It helped a lot more than I expected it to."

"I guess we'll be attending a lot of funerals before we die."

Leanne nodded. "I guess so. But we'll also have a lot of friends, and a lot of happy times. Maybe even fall in love."

"Would you let yourself? Knowing that you'd never be able to grow old together?"

Leanne frowned. "You know what? I don't think you can stop it. I don't think it's much of a choice. I never chose to love you."

Casey hooked her arm into Leanne's. "I'm glad you did though. Now we're sisters. Forever."

"Not quite forever."

They walked on in silence, the spring sun warming their backs.

"Do you think they created any kind of afterlife for us?" Casey asked. "Do you think we'll see everyone we ever love there someday?"

Leanne smiled. "Despite everything, I'm choosing to believe so."

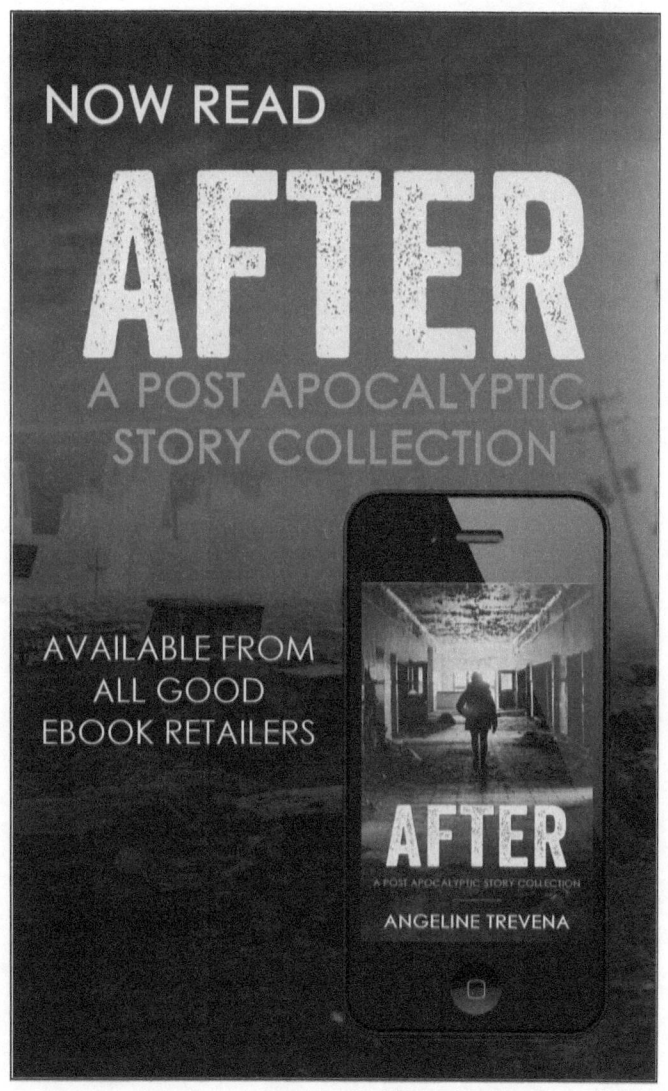

ACKNOWLEDGEMENTS

Writing this book has been quite an unusual experience. Not only is the post-apocalyptic genre a break from my usual dose of dystopia and urban fantasy, but setting a book in our world, rather than an imagined one, has been fun and different. Although Chatstone and Horraton are imaginary places, the England they're set in is very real, and I was restricted by the possibilities of that.

And so, my first thank you is to my husband who patiently, and without judgement, answered a host of random questions about things like mobile phone masts, and army lingo. As well as "Does weedkiller smell?"

He is my rock, my anchor, and the only thing that brings me back down to earth when I get my head into a muddle (which happens all too often).

And then there are my boys. I can't ever say that they actually help me with my writing, they are, if anything, a hindrance, but I wouldn't change things. They're the reason I get up in the morning (quite literally!), and their needs keep me anchored in the real world, saving me from floating off, never to be seen again, into my fictional imaginings.

Although I'll be glad to put the entire saga of the

broken leg behind us, part of this book was written, and thought about (because thinking is as much a part of writing as actual writing is) at a hospital bedside, and in between, what now feels like, countless hospital visits. So, in part, I must dedicate this book to the wonderful staff of our local hospital, and the tireless amazingness of the NHS. Thank you for the use of your table, your electricity, and the soft, ambient lighting during my (very) early morning writing sessions.

To the endless generosity of my mother-in-law who, basically, gave up her entire summer to take care of my eldest son, while I looked after the one in the plaster cast. You made this summer bearable, and possible.

And to my own parents. While we didn't get our usual seaside holiday with you, your house is always a sanctuary for my poor, tired brain. As much as writers need to be chained to their desks, they also need wide spaces for roaming, and you offer me that in abundance, both figuratively and literally. You are my open space. You're also a generous source of cake.

As ever, a thank you goes to Oliviaprodesign for knocking yet another book cover out of the park.

And the critical eyes, and generous honesty, of Kay Smillie, Pat Salvant, Nigel Perels, and Monica Lewallen. You make me better, sharper, and acutely aware of my failings. At the same time, you boost my confidence in ways you can't even imagine. Your kind words spur me on, to write more, to write better, to try and reign in those damn commas.

And finally, because I appear to have rambled onto a third page with this, I want to thank you, my readers. This book wouldn't exist without you. Leanne and Joel wouldn't exist without you. This whole adventure wouldn't.

And we have so many more adventures to go on together.

ABOUT ANGELINE TREVENA

Angeline Trevena was born and bred in a rural corner of Devon, but now lives among the breweries and canals of central England with her husband, their two sons, and a rather neurotic cat. She is a horror and fantasy author, poet, and journalist.

In 2003 she graduated from Edge Hill University, Lancashire, with a BA Hons Degree in Drama and Writing. During this time she decided that her future lay in writing words rather than performing them.

Some years ago she worked at an antique auction house and religiously checked every wardrobe that came in to see if Narnia was in the back of it. She's still not given up looking for it.

Find out more at www.angelinetrevena.co.uk